James Payn

Halves

Vol. 1

James Payn

Halves
Vol. 1

ISBN/EAN: 9783337047474

Printed in Europe, USA, Canada, Australia, Japan

Cover: Foto ©Andreas Hilbeck / pixelio.de

More available books at **www.hansebooks.com**

HALVES.

A Novel.

BY

JAMES PAYN,

AUTHOR OF "LOST SIR MASSINGBERD," "WALTER'S WORD,"
ETC. ETC.

In Three Vols.

VOL. I.

London:
TINSLEY BROTHERS, 8, CATHERINE ST., STRAND.
1876.

CHARLES DICKENS AND EVANS,
CRYSTAL PALACE PRESS.

CONTENTS.

CHAPTER I.

PAGE

THE RECTOR AND HIS WIFE 1

CHAPTER II.

MY SECRET 24

CHAPTER III.

OUR LITTLE DINNER-PARTY 44

CHAPTER IV.

A REVELATION 70

CHAPTER V.

AN ARRIVAL 90

CHAPTER VI.

PAGE

BROTHER ALEC 104

CHAPTER VII.

A NIGHT ALARM 137

CHAPTER VIII.

IN THE GARDEN 153

CHAPTER IX.

THE STORY OF UNCLE ALEC 170

CHAPTER X.

ALEC'S CONFESSION 191

CHAPTER XI.

MARK TAKES COURAGE 214

CHAPTER XII.

A CHANGE OF TREATMENT 226

CHAPTER XIII.

THE ACCUSATION 247

HALVES.

HALVES.

CHAPTER I.

THE RECTOR AND HIS WIFE.

IF the hills of Stanbrook were not dwarfed by the vicinity of the Westmoreland mountains, and its mere reduced to fairy proportions by the neighbourhood of the northern lakes, it would have a name for the picturesque, which at present it does not possess. You may have a very pretty property in land of your own, and one which would make you a "ground swell" in an open county, but if you happen to have a Beaufort or a Derby for neighbours, you are not greatly thought of; and as with people so with places. No one was ever invited by advertisement to take a return ticket to Stanbrook, at five shillings less per head if applied for on the previous day; no splendid picture, bathed in the dyes of sunset and magenta, ever portrayed that paradise at a railway station; nor was the British public ever invited by the *genius loci* (who generally keeps an inn) to "spend a happy day" there. Yet happy days were spent there for all that.

With all respect for the purveyors of travelling for the million, perhaps our very happiest days are not those which we enjoy in companies of from fifty to five hundred. In boyhood, indeed, it may be so; but in adolescence (or even later) two is the better number; while, in mature age, it is well to wander over some fair scene alone, and think, with unbidden but not unhappy tears, of those who once shared with us its pleasures, and are fled to that "city glorious," that "great and distant city," planned on a scale of which no Board of Works has ever dreamed.

Oh, rare and pure is the breeze upon the hill-top, and cool and pure the breeze upon the mere; but when they breathe for us a gracious memory, they are airs no more of earth, but blow from heaven!

Ah, little house, still mine, but emptied of its pride! Ah, quiet churchyard that enfolds it all, forbear to glass yourselves in these dewy eyes; I turn from Death to Life, from Now to Then, and strive to draw a picture from the Past!

It is an autumn morning; the mists have left the bases of the hills, but shroud their summits; above is the sea of vapour, save one broad peninsula of light that strikes upon a little garden, and decks its trees with drops of diamonds, and sows its lawn with pearls and rubies, and breaks upon the lake in flame. It flames, too, upon the window of the breakfast parlour, so that Aunt Eleanor, seated at the urn, cries, "What a glare! do draw the blind down, Harry."

But cried Uncle Ralph : "Nay, never shut God's sunshine out in autumn. Let me wheel your chair round ; so, my dear. If you knew how light became you and your rings" (here he cast a glance at me, that twinkled with sly humour as brightly as the rings themselves), "you'd have no shade— except to cast your rivals into."

"You are pleased to be facetious this morning, Mr. Hastings," was my aunt's stiff reply; but she took his speech in good part, notwithstanding. It was impossible to put Aunt Eleanor out by any overdose of compliment. She was near upon threescore years and ten, and had been a very fine woman in her day, which, in her own opinion, was by no means over yet. Her complexion was still that of a young girl ; her dark hair, which was but slightly tinged with grey, was as plentiful as that of most girls, and it was all her own. She was indebted neither to the rhinoceros nor vegetable ivory for a single tooth. Her hands were a marvel for her age,

so plump, and white, and small ; and if there
were some nodosities about the knuckles, they
served the better to keep her rings on. I
doubt whether any woman had ever seen my
Aunt ·Eleanor, without wondering who would
have those rings when she came to die—a
reflection which never troubled the good lady
herself in the least. Perhaps (trusting to her
knuckles) she had an idea they would be
buried with her, and that she might make
a figure with them in other spheres ; or,
more probably, the subject was altogether
foreign to her thoughts. She had had a
life interest in forty thousand pounds so
long, that I think it had moulded her character, and made her averse to speculations
about the future.

Do not let it be supposed, however,
that Aunt Eleanor was irreligious. Far from
it. Indeed, she would scarcely have married
a clergyman—for Uncle Ralph was the rector
of Stanbrook—had that been the case. Moreover, although an essentially worldly woman,

she had many good qualities; and, though so vain, plenty of wits. It was said, indeed —but mostly by ladies (who, I venture to think, are not infallible judges on such a point)—that she had more common sense in her little finger (the only one without the rings) than her husband had in his whole body. *Omne ignotum pro magnifico* is no more invariably true than other proverbs; and Uncle Ralph was a humorist. A more kindly undesigning creature than he never existed; and the wonder was how he had ever committed the prudence of marrying my aunt—a lady ten years older than himself, it is true, but in all other respects so excellent a match. My own conviction is, that he had had but little voice in the matter. Up to nearly forty years of age Eleanor Raby had been walking the wood looking for a straight stick, when it suddenly struck her that she must not be so particular, and the Rev. Ralph Hastings happening to fall in her way, she had picked him up and appropriated him.   He was wholly unsuspicious of her design, imagining her to be meat for his masters—much too high on Fortune's ladder for the likes of him; but, so soon as he was made to understand the necessity of the case, his good nature compelled him to succumb.   He had but three thousand pounds of his own, and his so-called living, which brought him in two hundred a year, the half of which he paid back to the poor of the parish; the rectory itself had been but a poor cottage, till, under my aunt's golden reign, it had blossomed into as bright "a bijou residence" as English sun e'er shone on.   She had spent more money on the house than would have built it ten times over; the very room in which we sat had had a window "let in" over the fireplace, which the architect had pronounced to be "an impossibility," and charged for it accordingly when surmounted; and to sit with her small feet on the fender, watching the snow fall on the Fells, and reflecting that

she had had her will in spite of that architect,
was one of my aunt's winter pleasures. Her
mother had been a Frenchwoman, and she
ought to have been French herself by rights,
so tasteful and trim she was, so shallow and
sparkling, so sentimentally tender, and so
childishly selfish. There were only three
persons in the world, beside herself, for whom
she had any personal affection, I believe, at
the time of which I write : first, her husband
—I have a doubt of his being first, but I
give him and her the benefit of it; secondly,
her Blenheim spaniel, Nelly, who was "a
great invalid," as her mistress was wont to
say, and pushed the wants and caprices of
invalidism to extremity ; and, thirdly, though
at a considerable interval, her nephew and
biographer, myself.

"Harry, boy, you don't eat," said my
uncle; "what is the matter?"

"Why need you ask, Mr. Hastings? He
has had but a trout and two eggs, and a
little cold beef, it is true, at present; but

then, don't you remember that to-morrow he leaves us?"

"Pull down the blind," said my uncle, sententiously; and this time I obeyed him at once.

"There, now," continued my aunt, patting my shoulder graciously, "I am no longer angry with anybody, and least of all with you, Harry. Let me have my own way, and I am always delighted. I am very sorry you are going away. If your uncle had not been so cruel, you might have remained here all your days—at least, all *my* days—and written poems to the sunsets. For my part, I would like you to be a poet, and nothing else. It is so ethereal; now that is not at all the case with an attorney."

"Very likely," remarked my uncle; "but unless Harry is poet enough to live, as Eve Fleigon of Clere did, on no other nourishment than the smell of flowers—"

"How delightful!" interposed my aunt.

"In summer time, perhaps; but when it

came to the dahlia season I should not have envied her. Well, since Harry has nothing to depend upon but his own exertions, it is necessary he should set to work.

" How sad ! " sighed my aunt.

" He has had the education of a gentleman at the University," continued the rector, looking towards his wife, but in reality, as I was well aware, intending his discourse for my private behoof; "and I much regret that he did not get more out of it. You have heard of a man being ' a gentleman and a scholar ; ' well, unhappily, he did not become the latter. You have also heard of the alternative of being ' a gentleman ' or ' a fellow ; ' he, unfortunately, chose the former. Worse than all, he has elected to devote his time and talents to the . composition of verse, for which he will never get a farthing a foot—not alcaic, but linear measure."

" Nay, he got two guineas for that charming valentine in the *Illustrated Post* last February," interposed my aunt, good-naturedly.

"Well, let us except the valentine; a man who can only make money by his profession on the 14th of February reminds one of the American gentleman whose calling was to blacken glasses against eclipse days. Harry Sheddon will never be the Laureate, nor even procure bread and cheese by his muse. What profession would he choose then, was the question which I, as his guardian, was bound to put to him. He has answered, 'I will be an attorney. I will be articled to Mr. Mark Raeburn, at Kirkdale. It is but ten miles away, so that I can run over to Stanbrook and see you and my aunt every Saturday if you wish it.' Of course we wish it. The arrangement is most welcome to me every way, and shows in the boy as much good feeling as good sense."

"And these Raeburns—these wretches who are depriving us of our Harry—are coming to dinner to-day, are they not?" inquired my aunt.

"Certainly; the coach has just stopped at the gate to leave the fish, no doubt."

"Well, I suppose I must make myself agreeable to them."

"Nay, my dear, that is unnecessary. Nature has taken that trouble off your shoulders—you have only to be your charming self. The Raeburns are not much in your way, it must be owned."

"Ah, I know them," said my aunt, with a little shudder. "The man is not so bad, indeed, except for marrying the woman. He must have committed great crimes, however, to have deserved her."

"No, no, Mark is a good fellow," laughed my uncle; "you can't judge of desert by marriages, else what an angel must I be to have been rewarded with such a prize as you, my dear. He is an excellent fellow, and as straight as a die; my only fear is that he has not quite enough business to teach Harry his trade. Mrs. Raeburn is a terrible woman, I allow, and sets one's teeth on edge to look at her. I wouldn't kiss her for a fifty-pound note."

"Indeed, I hope not," said my aunt, with a toss of her head; "and I hope Harry won't. One thing is certain, if he does, he will never get another kiss from his Aunt Eleanor."

"Then I am quite sure he won't," remarked my uncle, with confidence. "Moreover, she would never give the fifty-pound note; she is a thorough skinflint. To see her pay away a shilling is a most piteous spectacle; it makes her look as if she was drawing out one of her finger-nails. You must give Harry some provisions to take away—jams, and hams, and so forth, as you did when he was going to school, else I'm certain he'll be starved. She starves her own son John; no young fellow of his age could look so gaunt, and grim, and old, if he were not starved."

"How can you think of going to live among such people, Harry?" inquired my aunt, throwing up her jewelled hands. "It is dreadful even to think that they are coming to dinner."

"Well, I rather like Mr. Raeburn, aunt," said I, cheerfully; "and John is a clever fellow, and a most excellent mimic."

"Mimic! who is there to mimic at Kirkdale?" asked my aunt, contemptuously.

I felt very hot and uncomfortable; for, the very last time I had met John Raeburn, he had personated my respected aunt, even to that very manner of her throwing up her head, with an accuracy that had drawn tears of laughter from me.

"Oh, everybody about," said I, carelessly; "his father and mother, for instance, and the new doctor, Mr. Wilde."

"Nice, dutiful boy!" observed my uncle. "However, they are all coming to dinner, and Miss Floyd with them."

"Miss Floyd!" exclaimed my aunt; "who is Miss Floyd?"

"Why, surely I told you about her?" said my uncle, in some confusion; "she is Mark Raeburn's ward, and, I believe, his cousin. When I took your invitation to the Briary——"

"The Priory, Uncle Ralph," suggested I.

"Yes, I know it is the Priory, but it ought to be the Briary, so I always call it so; a wilderness of a place, like the garden of the sluggard, and everything sharp, and prickly, and disagreeable about it. Not," added he, hastily, "but that Harry will find himself quite at home there, no doubt, in time."

"But about this Miss Floyd?" insisted my aunt; "for this is the first time I ever heard of her from either of you."

"Well, Harry ought to have told you, though I forgot it, since he knows all about her."

"My dear uncle!" remonstrated I.

"Knows all about her!" repeated my aunt, "and has never told me a word!"

"This is quite a mistake, Aunt Eleanor," stammered I. "I have seen the young lady once or twice, it is true, but as to forgetting that she was to come to dinner, I don't see what right Uncle Ralph has to shift the blame to my shoulders. When he took your note of invitation to Mrs. Raeburn, with an apology for your not calling in person, she was rather inclined to be offended — drew herself up——"

"Quite unnecessary," interposed my aunt; "she's always like a ramrod."

"Well, you see, you had never visited her, and perhaps it struck her that you would not have asked her to dinner if I had not been about to be articled to her husband."

"Therein she showed her sagacity," was my aunt's quiet comment.

"Well, at all events, that made her stiff as buckram, and she told Uncle Ralph that it would have given herself and Mr. Raeburn very great pleasure to dine at Stanbrook, but that his cousin Miss Floyd was residing with them——"

" No, no," interrupted my uncle, laughing ; " you are spoiling the story. She said that they would be happy to come, but that there was her son John."

" 'Then bring him,' said I ; ' we have plenty of room ;' and, indeed, we had agreed, you know, to ask him."

" 'Nay, but there is Miss Floyd,' said she."

" Mercy on us !" cried my aunt ; " I wonder you did not invite a dozen of them."

" Well, my dear, you see it was like the fable of the fox, and the goose, and the bushel of corn. She couldn't leave Miss Floyd alone—the prettiest girl, by-the-by, I've seen for many a day—and she couldn't leave her Don Juan of a son at home—you'll think him exceedingly like Don Juan—to

keep company with her, so that, having
once mentioned the young fellow's name, I
had to ask them all four. It's only once
and away, you know, and it will make them
civil to the lad here. Then, having business
matters to settle with Raeburn, the whole
affair escaped my recollection. Besides, I
made sure, since Harry was present, that he
would have told you all about it.—Well,
Richard, what's the matter ?"

"Oh, please, sir, the fish !" exclaimed
the man-servant, who had approached my
aunt with a frightened look, as though
about to make a confession of some calamity,
and now gladly turned towards my uncle,
"there has something happened to the
salmon."

"Something happened ! What do you
mean, man ? Has it caught the small-pox ?
Bring it in, and let's look at it."

"Not in here, I beg," observed my
aunt. "Take it into the porch, Richard, and
show it to your master. No, don't you

move, Harry ; I want to have a word with you."

I would very gladly have accompanied my uncle, but of course there was no escaping this direct command. I kept my seat, therefore, and looked up at my aunt with an air of as innocent surprise as it was possible to assume in such an emergency.

"So, nephew, you have embraced the profession of the law, have you, to please Mr. Hastings, and because, by doing so, you would be within reach of your dear uncle and aunt ? "

" Those were some of the reasons, Aunt Eleanor."

" They are all that I have heard mentioned—that is, directly," observed the old lady, with meaning. " But it seems the law has other attractions for you ? "

" Not many, that I am aware of," answered I, with a feeble laugh.

" Don't giggle," was my aunt's reproving rejoinder. " That is a girl's trick, which I

conclude you have caught from this young
person already. You need not look so
simple. How old are you, sir?"

"I am just twenty-one."

"Well, at twenty-one a man does not
forget that 'the prettiest girl one has seen
for many a day' is coming to dinner; I
doubt even whether your uncle did. You
didn't dare to tell me about her. She is
doubtless a vulgar creature, of whom you
are enamoured and yet ashamed."

"I am not ashamed of her. She has
nothing to be ashamed of," cried I, rising
from the chair and speaking with indignant
vehemence. "She is as ladylike and accomplished as she is beautiful."

"Oh, Lud, it's as bad as that, is it,
Harry?" cried my aunt—then burst into one
of her rare fits of mirth, that sounded like
the tinkling of sledge-bells. "Well, well,
it's very natural, and a great pity that such
little dears can't marry and settle in a doll's
house at once. Has she any money, child?"

"I don't know," said I, with sullen sheepishness.

Then the silver laughter rose again and fell all about me like a fountain-song.

"Of course he doesn't know!" cried she, admiringly. "It would have been out of all keeping had he made inquiries about so superfluous a matter. Ah, youth! Ah, love! Ah, me!" A look of inexpressible sadness—the reflection, perhaps, of her own past, swept over her furrowed face. She laid a sparkling hand upon my shoulder, and in a voice in which the shrillness of old age was rendered musical by tenderness, said, "Leave all to me, Harry. If the girl is worthy of you, and I like her, you shall embrace—your profession."

I took her hand—to squeeze it was impossible, because of the rings—and raised it to my lips.

"Confusion!" cried she, with the accent of a Dejazet; "my husband!"

At that moment my uncle had re-entered

the room, with a purple face and a fish basket. He held his disengaged hand to his side, and appeared half suffocated with laughter.

"Never," gasped he, "since the world was made—never, at least, since the water was peopled—has such a sight been seen as this. Look at it, Eleanor!"

My aunt raised her double eye-glasses, and gazed into the basket with a supercilious air. "I see a large crab and a fish bone."

"Yes, a very large crab — a crab that weighs six pounds more than he did when he left town—and the bone of a salmon. The crab has boned that salmon."

"What, eaten it on the way?"

"Most certainly he has. It is magnificent! What martyr doomed to execution has ever shown such calmness, what hero such presence of mind?"

"Well, we have the salmon still," observed my aunt with satisfaction, "since it is inside the crab."

"My dear Eleanor, I am shocked at you; that is the reflection of a political economist. Harry, put your hat on; there is the dog-cart at the door. I must request you to drive this gentleman to Morecambe Bay, and put him carefully into the sea again—somewhere in the sand, where he will be able to be quiet and digest at leisure."

"But, my dear uncle——"

"Yes, I am sorry to trouble you," interrupted the rector, gravely, "but I couldn't trust him to Richard. He would only pretend to throw him in, as Sir Bedivere pretended to throw the sword Excalibur, and sell him to somebody for half-a-crown. A crab like that is worth his weight in gold, and shall never be eaten if I can help it."

So I drove the crab to Morecambe that morning—a good eight miles—and restored him to his native element.

CHAPTER II.

MY SECRET.

My aunt was right in her view of what had been the magnet that had drawn me towards the legal profession. I had no particular liking for the law itself, nor, to say truth, for any profession. Though far from illiterate, I was by nature indolent, and disinclined to application of any sort. The Church, the Bar, the Army, had each been presented for my choice in turn by my good uncle, after his peculiar manner; not point-blank, as more business-like guardians would have put them, but in a half-playful, half-serious fashion. "Archbishop, Lord Chancellor, Field-Marshal; come, which shall it be, Harry?"

He had never pressed the question home, partly because he was himself as indolent as I, and partly because he was averse to lose me. I had never grown weary of Stanbrook, but passed all my vacations there in great content. I loved the great green fells, the silver mere; I shot, I rode, I fished; and had enough of geniality of my own to appreciate the rector's humour. We liked each other's company; and though he knew the time was come for me to put my armour on, and mix in the *mêlée* of the world, he kept me with him, and I was glad to stay. I was his companion everywhere, and helped him all I could. In church I read the lessons for him; at the Sunday-school I took a class beyond my powers, lest his own knowledge concerning the kings of Judah should be put to too severe a test; and when he went into Kirkdale, weekly, to the Petty Sessions, it was I who drove his dog-cart.

It was on one of these occasions—though

not at the Petty Sessions—that I had first met Gertrude Floyd. She was walking arm-in-arm with her cousin, John Raeburn, who introduced her to me ; and my first thought, as I well remember, was what an ill-assorted pair they were. For John was short for a man, and thin and grim, though his features had great flexibility, and were capable, as I have said, of simulating the expression of persons widely differing from himself; and Miss Floyd was tall, though daintily shaped, and beautiful exceedingly ; and yet, I swear, it was not her beauty—not the rippling fall of her brown hair, which flowed unrestrainedly from under her summer hat ; nor the liquid gentleness that shone in her hazel eyes ; nor the whiteness of her low broad brow ; nor the colour, like that which tips the daisy, that adorned her cheeks—that made me hers from that eventful hour—but her gracious looks. She had a smile for everybody, not the simper that some girls wear, in acknow-ledgment of the admiration they are anxious of inviting, but a sort of heavenly radiance; as the genial sun shines both upon the just and the unjust, so did she seem to smile both on me and John. There are men who would have blamed her for that; but I felt no pang of jealousy. It was clear to me that, out of her charity and tenderness, she looked thus kindly on her cousin—who was nothing (or at least very little) to look at; while something whispered to my beating heart that I had already found favour in her eyes. It was very egotistic in me—very conceited, it may even be said—but there is no need to argue upon that subject, because, as the event proved, I was right.

"This is Mr. Sheddon," said John, with his crooked smile—he always smiled from one side of his face, and I felt a great inclination on the present occasion to make him smile upon the other—"Mr. Harry Sheddon, the poet."

You may imagine the tone in which a budding attorney in a country town would make such an observation as that; it was with the intention, of course, of making me ridiculous in the eyes of his fair companion. I had had the imprudence to publish a small volume of immature verse, and what is true of a prophet in his own country was eminently so of a poet in Kirkdale. You can imagine, therefore, I say, the tone of Mr. John Raeburn; but you cannot imagine, unless you have heard a chorus of nightingales by daytime, the exquisite music of Miss Floyd's voice as she replied:

"I have read Mr. Sheddon's poems with great pleasure." If we had been alone, I should doubtless have found fit words to acknowledge this compliment; but with Mr. John Raeburn standing by, I showed an embarrassment with which he was pleased to make very merry.

When he saw that I was really annoyed, however, he desisted. "Come," said he, "your uncle has got a long case at the sessions-house, and will not be out these

two hours. Why not look in on us at the
Priory ? We have had our luncheon," added
he, naïvely, as though, if that meal had yet
to come, the circumstance would have been
an insuperable obstacle to the invitation, as
indeed it doubtless would. The Raeburns
were not famous for their hospitality. When
they gave a dinner-party, it was said (for
I had had no personal experience of the
fact, since our families did not visit,
though my uncle had business relations with
the attorney) that, though champagne-glasses
were placed at each guest's side, the place
of the sparkling liquid was supplied in
summer time by flowers, in winter by Indian
grasses, which tickled the nose without
satisfying the palate. It was a favourite
story of the rector's, that he had once
extricated himself from the meshes of Mrs.
Raeburn's conversation in Kirkdale, by dash-
ing through the bridge toll-gate, whereby
an impassable gulf—since it involved the
payment of a halfpenny—had been placed

between them. And yet the attorney had a tolerable practice in the district, and was reported rich.

The Priory was an ancient mansion of some pretensions, standing a little outside the town, and possessing a large walled garden—so ill-kept, however, that it well deserved my uncle's name for it (the Briary) —in which the fruits and flowers bore but a small proportion to the vegetables. The house was surrounded by a grove of ragged elms, which gave it a gloomy appearance, and within, as I afterwards discovered, reigned a social gloom in every chamber, save those alone which Gertrude Floyd irradiated by her presence. Even on that first occasion it struck me that I had never seen a lady do the honours of her house with so ill a grace as Mrs. Raeburn. She was tall and big-boned, though flat and thin as a pancake, and had a hard, suspicious eye. Nature had evidently intended her to be mistress of a reformatory, or abbess of a convent, where the rules were of the severest kind ; but circumstances had restricted her sphere of usefulness and energy. She was one of those women, in short (of whom it must be owned there are a good many) who at once suggest the question to all beholders, " How could any man have married her ? " and when you saw her husband, this query was repeated, with a difference, " How could honest Mark Raeburn, of all men, have married her ? "

For the attorney, notwithstanding that he had passed some thirty years in the practice of his profession, had an honest, good-humoured face, which, though at this date careworn enough, must at one time have been the index of a cheery disposition ; and even now, when free from the chilling influence of his wife's presence, he was known to sing a good song with effect, and would drain his glass (with other people's wine in it) as freely as any man.

" So, so ; this is an unexpected pleasure,

Mr. Sheddon," said he, coming in from his office to the dining-room, with which it communicated by folding-doors, and shaking me cordially by the hand.

"An unexpected condescension, I call it," observed Mrs. Raeburn, grimly. "I have just been saying that Mrs. Hastings has never deigned to set foot in the Priory."

"My aunt is in very delicate health, my dear madam," stammered I, "and goes out scarcely anywhere."

"Of course, of course," said the attorney, hastily; "that's it, my dear, that's it. The rector is, I am sure, a constant visitor of ours——"

"On business," interpolated this inexorable woman.

"Well, well, on business or pleasure, it's all one. Perhaps Mr. Sheddon is here with an eye to business—thinks of being articled to me, perhaps, and becoming one of the family for the next five years; no, since he has taken his degree at the University, it will be only three. But he might do worse, much worse."

Up to that instant I had had no more idea of being articled to Mr. Mark Raeburn than of being a Christy Minstrel; but the phrase, " becoming one of the family," addressed to me, as it was, with beautiful Gertrude Floyd standing before my eyes, who I knew to be an inmate of the house, attracted me vastly.

" The fee would be three hundred guineas," remarked Mrs. Raeburn, as coolly as if she were asking me to take wine; which, however, she had shown no inclination to do.

" My dear, my dear! That's my affair," interposed the attorney, reprovingly; " a question to be settled between Mr. Sheddon's uncle and guardian and myself."

" The arrangement for his being here would be mine," continued Mrs. Raeburn, quite unruffled. " I could not think of taking less than one hundred and fifty guineas per annum, exclusive of wash-ing."

"And he must bring a silver fork and spoon with him, which will not be returned," observed John Raeburn, in a voice so like his mother's that the similarity made me shake with inward laughter, and even drew a suppressed chuckle from the attorney.

"John, leave the room!" cried Mrs. Raeburn; an order that he instantly obeyed by vanishing into the office. "You are, doubtless, unaccustomed, sir, to hear a mother mocked by her own flesh and blood?"

To this I made no reply, for I dared not trust myself to speak. It was a very common remark with her, as I afterwards discovered, when the irrepressible John ven- tured on any mimicry, and was perhaps made use of, in refutation of those persons, of whom there were many in Kirkdale, who affirmed that Mrs. Raeburn was not made of flesh and blood at all, but of cast-iron.

"My uncle has not yet come to any decision as to my future profession," observed I; "but I will be sure to tell him what you say, Mr. Raeburn."

"Do so; do, my lad; the rector's a great favourite of ours, and his nephew would be very welcome to our circle. Matilda, give him a glass of wine."

Mrs. Raeburn sighed, and produced the keys of the cellaret. "Will you have sherry wine, or sweet wine? In the middle of the day, perhaps, a glass of raisin——"

"No, no; sherry, sherry," interposed the attorney, impatiently; "gentlemen from the University do not drink home-made wines."

The hostess shook her head (which had a cap on trimmed with black bugles) in a hearse-like fashion, as much as to say, "So much the worse for them, and for their friends who have to pay their wine bills;" and unwillingly produced the decanter.

"Two glasses, my dear," said the

attorney; "no gentleman likes to drink alone."

Mrs. Raeburn muttered an ejaculation, partly of contempt, partly, perhaps, of incredulity—for, indeed, it was whispered that the attorney himself had by no means a disinclination to that practice—and produced a second glass. The action was fatal to her scheme of economy, for, while she turned, her husband seized the decanter, and took advantage of its possession not only to fill my glass up to the brim, but, presently, to help himself a second time, notwithstanding an audible groan of reproof from his consort.

" Here's to our better acquaintance, Mr. Sheddon. I have often regretted, for my son John's sake, that he saw so little of you. I am sorry that I have no leisure this morning to do the honours of the Priory; but Gertrude here will doubtless show you at least the garden."

Nothing could have been more consonant

with my wishes than this arrangement, as, doubtless, the attorney had foreseen. That unlooked-for proposal of my becoming one of his household would scarcely have been made, I fancy, had he not relied upon her attractions to make it welcome. Its abruptness was characteristic of his nature, and, so far from the proposition offending me, I even felt flattered by it, for it was absurd to suppose that the amount of my premium, or the few pounds a year his wife might make by my "keep," could be of moment to a man in his position.

Miss Floyd, however, I thought, looked pained and shamed. She led the way to the garden without a word, and when I remarked to her upon its beauty—for it was summer time, when even the wilderness is beautiful—she made no reply, but reverted to the previous topic.

"I hope, Mr. Sheddon," said she, "that you know my cousin well enough not to take all he says quite literally."

"Oh yes," replied I. "Everybody knows Mark Raeburn to be the most effusive of attorneys. What he must have been in his youth, before the chastening influence of his wife mitigated his enthusiasm——"

"For shame, Mr. Sheddon!" exclaimed my companion, smiling, however, in spite of herself; "I am sorry to find a satirist where I had expected a poet. Seriously, though, I do hope you will not repeat my cousin's proposition to your uncle."

I knew very well that she was alluding to the terms in which it had been made, so indicative of the greed of Mrs. Raeburn's nature, but I affected to misunderstand her.

"You have no wish, then, that I should be made one of the family at the Priory?"

"Nay, it would be as rude to say that as unbecoming to express the contrary. What concerns me more particularly in the matter is, that my kinsman should not be rendered ridiculous to others, by your representing the case as it actually occurred."

Then for the first time the truth flashed upon me. The attorney had been intoxicated. I recalled his flushed face and hurried accents; his having been at home that day, too, had not my mind been otherwise occupied, ought to have struck me with surprise, since he was clerk to the magistrates, and should have been in his place in the Sessions House. Miss Floyd had evidently given me credit for keener observation than I had possessed, and was now appealing to my good feeling, not to make her cousin's condition a public scandal. How sad it seemed that this pure and fair young creature should have to plead in such a cause, and that to a comparative stranger such as I! How melancholy must be her days, thought I, passed in such a house as this, among companions so ignoble! There was one way only by which it was in my power to ameliorate her lot—namely, by sharing it; by accepting, in sober seriousness, the offer that Mark Raeburn had made to me in his cups, and I at once resolved to do so. It was a rash and impulsive decision; but I had really, as I have said, no preference for one profession over another, and it had become absolutely necessary to make a choice. Moreover, there was the most beautiful girl I had ever beheld, appealing to me with dewy eyes, and in a voice which emotion had rendered tremulous. I was but twenty-one years of age, too, and a poet.

" I shall certainly come to the Priory," said I, in a rapture, " and use my most heartfelt endeavours "—I was about to add, " to mitigate your unhappy position," when her look of cold surprise checked me midway, and made me stammer in its place— " to become an attorney."

I had forgotten that the ardent thoughts which had flashed through my brain had done so without her knowledge, and that to her I must have seemed to be merely considering whether I should tell people

that her cousin Mark had had too much
wine, or should conceal the fact. " Of
course," I continued, " what has happened
to-day will never be repeated by me ; and
indeed, to say truth, Miss Floyd, I have
paid but little attention to it. It is no
flattery to say that in your presence——"

" You must bring a silver fork and
spoon, which will not be returned," croaked
Mrs. Raeburn close to my ear in the person
of her son John. " Don't flatter yourselves
that you were the only spectators of the
ratification of the treaty," he continued,
bursting into laughter. " I was watching
it all through the baize door ; I heard my
Dad evade the ginger wine and saw him collar
the sherry. Oh dear, oh dear, what a scene
it was ! "

Of course I had no further private talk
with the charming Gertrude. The quotations from the " Sensitive Plant," which I
had prepared in my mind for instant use,
à *propos* of the garden, had to be suppressed,

and nothing but the merest commonplaces could be indulged in.

But I was only the more resolved to seek other opportunities of speech with her, and that as soon as possible. Her voice haunted my ear throughout that day like wedding chimes; the touch of her hand, as she bade me simple farewell, lingered on it for hours and "filled my pulses with the fulness of the spring." From that day my rides had always Kirkdale for their object, and when I chanced to see her there, I came back radiant to the Rectory, to be congratulated by Aunt Eleanor on my high spirits, or rebuked for them, according to the state of her nerves. If I did not meet my charmer, I was as dull as ditchwater all the evening. But not a hint did I drop to any human creature of the cause of this rise and fall in my barometer, but hugged the precious secret to my heart as though it had been my Gertrude's self. My proposition of being articled to Mr. Raeburn, though utterly un-

expected by my uncle, was much too welcome to him for any expression of surprise,
and so it happened that, in but a week or
two from my first visit to the Priory, it
was arranged that I should become a resi-
dent there for the next three years; and
that, on the very day on which my story
opens, the Raeburn family, accompanied by
the object of my affections, were to be the
guests of my aunt and uncle at Stanbrook.

Little did I guess, from the intimacy
thus brought about by my own act, and
induced by love and youth, in what a net-
work of intrigue and fraud I was about to
be entangled.

CHAPTER III.

OUR LITTLE DINNER-PARTY.

I MUST have been very much in love in those days, for I remember that, throughout that long drive to Morecambe Bay, the absurdity of my errand—the fact that I had a large live crab in the dog-cart, which was neither to be eaten, nor sold, nor given away, but was to be placed on a retired plateau of sand, near stones, to which he might betake himself, if so inclined—did not occupy my mind, though humour was by nature welcome to it. I had laughed when my uncle had intrusted me with the task, and I laughed again when I had accomplished it: when the huge ungainly object of my care was squatting on the sand in front of me, so astonished to find himself there, instead of on a fishmonger's slab, that for a minute or two he could do nothing but stare and slobber, and presently, still staring, disappeared in the wet sand, in a grave of his own digging; but for the most part I thought of nothing but Gertrude. Did she like shell-fish, I wondered, and should I be able to afford to give it her when we were married? When those three years of apprenticeship should be over—no servitude like that which Jacob endured for his Rachel, but a blessed state of existence, since it would be passed in her society—and I should be a full-fledged attorney, and competent, if clients came, to mate with my angel. It would be necessary, perhaps, to live in a town, but in the summer time we should pass a month or two, at all events, in some beautiful district, such as that I was now traversing—perhaps that very one. Oh, to be driving her (instead of the crab) to the shore of the silver sea, that she might bathe there (a salt-water Undine), or to wander over the sparkling sands together (the sea-air could never make her bilious, as it did Aunt Eleanor); to be walking home with her along that very road, by moonlight, with my arm round her dainty waist, and naught but the silent hills—and those at a great distance—to watch our proceedings. I remember that drive for its sweet visions, as though I took it but yesterday, and how they were rudely broken in upon by the wheel of the dog-cart coming into contact with the fourth milestone—which reminded me of the distance on the road of life that yet lay between me and their accomplishment.

In later years I have talked of love to many men, and their first acquaintance with that passion, as related by themselves, has been something very different from my own. The view that the poets take of it, even in

youth, would seem to be a greatly exaggerated one, when tested by the common
experience. If his Belinda is unkind to a
man, he seeks consolation, not in vain, in
Betsey. Nay, Betsey present has as great
attractions for him as Belinda—kind—but
absent. Whether it was that I was really
something of a poet, or that Gertrude's
beauty was so superlative that no compa-
rison with that of others was possible, I
did certainly justify in my own case the
most extravagant assertions that have been
made concerning the power of love. There
were several young ladies in our neighbourhood who were more or less admired, and
about my "intentions" towards whom I had
been even rallied by Aunt Eleanor, but I
regarded them now with no more emotion
than if they had been of the other sex.
The very face of Nature was more fair to
me since I had seen Gertrude's; I beheld
her smile in the sunbeam, I felt her kisses
(though she had never kissed me) in the

summer breeze; and in the night I trembled with joy to think that she was but ten miles away. Imagine my transport then, in the reflection that that very evening she was coming to the Rectory, and that it would be my lot to take her in to dinner! I had never sat beside her yet; my eyes had never yet pastured on her fair face at leisure, as they might do a few hours hence, without reproof; there was a fragrance about her such as no scent could give, and it would encompass me; her dress would ripple over me; her round white arm would perchance touch mine. Bountiful Heavens!

I am told that some sensitive persons, even in middle age, experience similar emotions at the prospect of sitting by a lord! If so, I do not envy them. It was a sickening, swooney sensation after all, and for one thing, I remember well that it entirely destroyed my appetite. I dressed for dinner with infinite care and pains, but should not have taken half the time but

for the trembling of my limbs. The arrangement of my white cravat in particular was
a work of extreme difficulty, and I had as
many "failures" in it as Brummell. Then
I tottered down to the breakfast-room, which
commanded the approach to the house, and
flattened my nose against the window-pane
until the sudden thought struck me that I
was defacing that feature, which was ago-
nising. There was such a singing in my
ears that I did not hear the carriage till I
saw it at the door—a yellow "fly" from
the "George" at Kirkdale, about which no
pleasant associations had hitherto lingered,
for it had been wont to take me to school;
it was destined henceforth to be a sacred
vehicle.

"Harry!" cried my aunt's voice, from
the drawing-room, with which the breakfast-room communicated, "why on earth are
you not here, sir? Your uncle is not down,
and these people are your friends, remember,
not mine."

She had doubtless forgotten for the moment all about Gertrude, and was in no very pleasant frame of mind at having to welcome the Raeburns, whose acquaintanceship she had always studiously avoided. Otherwise, to my great envy, she was completely at her ease. I heard the shuffling of feet in the little hall, the sweeping of dresses (one of them *her* dress!), and a sharp " Stop a minute, Mark," from Mrs. Raeburn, whose cap perhaps had fallen on one side—what did it matter how she looked! Then the door opened, and Richard announced, "Mr., Mrs., and Mr. John Raeburn, and Miss Hoyd." I knew he had made some stupid mistake by John's giggle, but was too occupied with my duties as deputy-master of the ceremonies to hear what it was.

Aunt Eleanor welcomed Mrs. Raeburn with the most polished urbanity, to which that lady responded by an acid smile; properly speaking, she had no mouth at all, but only a slit between her nose and chin, which it seemed to give her pain to widen. "So glad to see you," said my aunt.

"So glad to see you, madam—after so many years," was the unconciliatory response.

"Yes," sighed my aunt, quite unabashed, "ill-health has deprived me of many pleasures. I have been a prisoner—to the house at least—I may almost say for life."

I had not been very studious of the classics, but the phrase *splendide mendax* involuntarily occurred to me. My aunt had at one time been a woman of fashion, and had not forgotten her accomplishments.

"My husband's cousin and ward, Miss Floyd," continued Mrs. Raeburn. It seemed to my sensitive ear that she laid a particular emphasis on the word "ward," as though to imply that her hand was at the attorney's disposal.

"Very pleased to see you, my dear," was my aunt's gracious welcome; youth and beauty were always passports to her favour, which surely was to her credit, since she had herself once possessed and lost them.

Mr. Raeburn came up rubbing his hands, a little nervous, but with a cheerful smile. Mrs. Hastings did not consider him quite a gentleman, or one that was in his proper place as a guest in her drawing-room ; but, being there, he had nothing to complain of in his reception.

As for Mr. John (perhaps with the remembrance of his powers of mimicry in her mind), my aunt gave him but a couple of fingers, and a "How do you do, sir?" the manner and tone of which he afterwards reproduced to perfection.

We were all a little stiff and formal, till my uncle came down, whose genial influence thawed the social atmosphere ; and as, moreover, with a desperation that his sense of the duties of hospitality could have alone inspired, he at once laid himself yard-arm to yard-arm beside the majestic Mrs. Raeburn, and engaged her with volleys of small talk, I was able to get a few words with Gertrude. Then dinner was announced—it was always served to the moment at the Rectory—and she laid her little hand on my trembling arm, and we were wafted into the dining-room together, as on pinions. During soup time conversation languished, but when the fish period arrived my aunt explained the absence of the salmon with great applause.

"Capital, capital!" cried the attorney, helping himself to the sherry, which, in country fashion, stood on the table; "he must be a noble crab, as I daresay he will prove. For my part, I think that a dressed crab is as good a dish as a salmon."

"But I am sorry to say the crab is gone too," said my aunt ruefully. She was rather ashamed of the rector's eccentric benevolence, and had hoped to have been spared the relation of it.

"Ho, ho! so somebody ate him too, did he?" observed Mr. Raeburn; then catching the smile upon my face, he added, "It must have been a young digestion that tackled such a fellow as that, and I think I can guess whose it was."

"Yes," said I, "I made away with the whole of it."

Mrs. Raeburn gasped audibly, and laid down her knife and fork. "If this lad eats a crab with a salmon in it for luncheon," was her private reflection, "a hundred and fifty pounds a year is too little by half to charge for his keep."

"Why, you are quite a Jonah, Sheddon!" exclaimed the attorney, with some slight confusion of metaphor.

"No, no!" exclaimed my aunt, "my nephew didn't eat the crab. The fact is, my husband was so struck with the creature's pluck, as he termed it, that he actually sent Harry to put it back in Morecambe Bay."

"And did you?" inquired John Raeburn, with simplicity.

"Did he, sir?" exclaimed my aunt with indignation; "do you suppose he sold it for half-a-crown upon the sly, and kept the money?"

"How pleasant it must be to be rich enough to indulge oneself in such eccentricities," observed Mrs. Raeburn, coldly.

This observation annoyed my aunt, I could see, even more than the remark of Mr. John, but she made no reply.

"Well, the crab is in the bay, Mrs. Raeburn," said my uncle, turning a little red, "and will probably be caught and 'sent to Kirkdale, so that you will have the benefit of it after all."

"Oh, we don't indulge in such luxuries at the Priory, I do assure you," replied Mrs. Raeburn, shooting a significant glance in my direction, as much as to say, "so don't expect them, young man." "I must say, Mr. Hastings, that I think you committed a wicked extravagance."

"I don't see why you must say it, my

dear," expostulated Mr. Raeburn, "even if you think it."

"I always speak my mind, Mark, as you know," was his lady's stern rejoinder, at which the attorney sighed, and again resorted to the sherry.

"For my part, I think it was very nice of your uncle," whispered Gertrude, timidly, "though it was certainly very funny."

This observation enchanted me, independently of its sentiments; for, since she said that it was funny, I was clearly privileged to smile in adhesion, and also to reply in the same hushed and tender key. How the general conversation proceeded from henceforth I took no note; but it struck me that there were gaps and pauses in it, and that every time Mr. Raeburn spoke it was with an access of confidence and gaiety. The champagne-glasses at Stanbrook Rectory were neither filled with Indian grasses nor suffered to stand empty before its guests.

I was sometimes addressed by others, of

course, in which case I answered them civilly
enough, but not without an effort; I could
not readily detach my mind from my divinity.
Once, for instance, I replied, " Beautiful!"
when Mr. Raeburn asked me what I thought
of the new medical man at Kirkdale, Dr.
Wilde. But whenever Gertrude was spoken
to I was all ears, and it did not escape me
that John Raeburn twice addressed her as
" Miss Hoyd," in allusion to our Richard's mistake in her introduction—a jocularity which,
considering that that domestic was waiting
at table, filled me with unspeakable disgust.

John was one of those anomalous indivi-
duals who, though really clever and quick-
witted, are wholly without discrimination;
vulgar he was to the backbone, and, what
was worse, he was absolutely unaware when
a pleasantry was calculated to give offence.
Nervous persons—and especially ladies—who
knew John, grew hot all over when, after a
preparatory grin, he opened his mouth for
a sally; and many and many a time have I

wished him choked. Such slapdash humorists, the oracles of their "office," or of the "commercial room," bring humour itself into disrepute, just as some pious folks, who have more zeal than knowledge, do discredit to true religion.

I am afraid I must have become more and more enrapt with my fair neighbour, since, when she suddenly whispered "Hush," I replied, "Why hush?" and the next instant was turned into stone by my aunt's "Harry! Grace!" for it seemed I had been interrupting the rector in that function. Moreover, when the ladies rose to go, I was wholly unprepared for it, having missed the stately bow interchanged between the hostess and Mrs. Raeburn, and did not fly to open the door for them, as was my bounden duty: from which occurred the absurdest circumstance, for John Raeburn, either from politeness, or to contrast his chivalry with my neglect, rushed at what he thought was the door and opened a cupboard full of jam-pots, kept there because the preserve-closet was damp—a revelation which annoyed my aunt beyond all measure.

Amongst us men, however, there was a roar of laughter, and we sat down to our wine in high good-humour. Though I would infinitely rather at once have "joined the ladies," I felt that my behaviour to Miss Floyd had been already somewhat exclusive, and was quite resolved to make up for it, by making myself pleasant to my uncle's guests; for which, indeed, little credit was due to me, since they had been invited solely upon my own account. Mr. John, too, by no means cast down by his fiasco with the cupboard, and evidently relieved by the absence of the ladies, chuckled over his walnuts with a gusto that could not have been exceeded if he had been an ape, and had stolen them; while the attorney manifested an hilarious garrulity which, even had Miss Floyd's appeal to me concerning him on the occasion of our first interview never been made, I could not fail to have attributed to the effects of liquor. He was not indeed what even the most ill-natured could have termed intoxicated; but the professional caution for which, despite his good-humour, he was rather remarkable, had vanished before the genial hospitality of my uncle, and also perhaps from his sense of satisfaction at finding himself a welcome guest at Stanbrook.

Mr. Hastings was not only personally very popular in the county, but his marriage with my aunt had given him a certain social position and importance, much beyond that commonly enjoyed by a country rector; and though singularly free from pretence or pride, his wife had compelled him to behave with a certain exclusiveness, which had kept such families as the Raeburns at a distance, and would without doubt have continued to do so, but for the accident of my electing to be an attorney-at-law. Thus Mr. Raeburn felt "elevated" in more than one sense, while his host's genuine kindness of manner warmed him into frankness and confidence. The sherry at the Priory was far from first-rate, nor was the key of the cellar easily attainable from the lady who was so good as to take charge of it, so that it was the custom of the attorney to make "a wet night" of it, whenever he had a favourable opportunity, while the absence of his wife and master always gave him a certain elasticity. His geniality, however, generally evaporated very harmlessly in a smoking or drinking song—a safety-valve unfortunately denied to him on the present occasion. He seldom lost his professional wariness; and never, as his son afterwards assured me, had he been so communicative—and that, too, with respect to his own affairs—as on that evening over the rector's mahogany. We were speaking, as was natural, about the law and its prospects, when some guarded expression of opinion on the attorney's part caused my uncle to rally him upon his caution. "Directly one touches on the subject of your profession, Raeburn, I notice that you shrink into your shell. In one so prosperous and trusted as yourself, I cannot understand such reticence—though, of course, in an incapable or 'shakey' practitioner, it would be explicable enough. When one speaks of military matters to a soldier, it is as though he heard the call of a trumpet, and his tongue is loosened instantly. Talk to my Harry here about poetry, and he will astonish you with his eloquence. But you lawyers seem always afraid of letting some cat-out-of-the-bag."

"We don't like giving advice gratis, you see, my dear sir," answered the attorney, slily, yet with a somewhat disconcerted and embarrassed air; "or, perhaps," added he, "we are afraid lest we should make the law intelligible to laymen, and that the familiarity should breed contempt."

"Upon my life, I do think there's something in that," replied my uncle, frankly. "You hedge about every legal operation with forms and ceremonies, such as would become an act of fetish-worship, rather than a transaction between civilised men, and hide your meaning in such a wearisome labyrinth of terms and phrases, that everyone shrinks from exploring it; and then you affect to wonder how sensible men can be ignorant of their own affairs. Wherever there is designed obscurity, I must confess it is my conviction that there is always more or less of imposture."

"That is pretty well for a clergyman, and a steward of divine mysteries," answered the attorney, roguishly.

"Nay, nay, I was only speaking of mundane matters," said my uncle; and then, with a pleasant smile, as if to condone his momentary gravity, he added, "besides, I have never heard a clergyman—at all events in the pulpit—accused of reticence. Now when you are in *your* pulpit you have not a word to say. It's the training that has done it—and on that account I fear it for my boy here, lest he should lose his frankness. Why, thirty years ago, Raeburn, I remember you as open as the day, just like your poor brother Alec."

"Aye, aye, rector, that is true enough," answered the attorney. "Thirty—years—ago." He drained his glass of port, and sighed deeply.

"He was your elder brother, if I remember right, was he not?" inquired my uncle, tenderly.

"He was, though we might have been almost twins for our likeness to one another, both in feeling and feature; but if he were alive now, it is likely, as you say, that our dispositions would be as different as the Poles. No one would believe, who did not know me then, of what enthusiasm of affection I was capable. If the details of our last interview should be written down, they would be thought too fanciful for a romance. Poor Alec!"

"You have never heard of him from that day to this, have you, Mark?"

"Never, Hastings, never. It is my own conviction that he died within a very few months of our parting. That took place at Liverpool, from which he sailed next day to America, to seek his fortune; for each of us had then to seek it. Not even my young friend Harry, yonder, with his taste for novel-reading and verse-writing, would ever guess the resolve that Alec and I arrived at on that occasion."

The air and manner of the attorney had become altogether altered while he thus spoke, and his tone had a pathos of which I had not conceived it capable.

"I think I can guess," said I, not without a feeling of secret triumph at my own sagacity; "you made an agreement with him that whoever should die first should appear to the other, and inform him of the fact !"

"Not so," answered the attorney gravely, "for what my brother promised he would have performed, and in that case I should have beheld him long ago. No, it was no spiritual compact, but a material one, and yet of so fanciful a nature that it might well pertain to another world than ours. We solemnly vowed to one another that, when we met again, we should make common lot of our fortunes—should divide in equal parts whatever property we might have both acquired in the interim."

A shrill whistle, which made my uncle "jump," dissolved the silence that followed this remarkable statement.

"I beg your pardon, sir," exclaimed John Raeburn, "but I couldn't help it. Only imagine how awkward it would be, if Uncle Alec was to come back with only a stick and a bundle, saying 'Divide, divide,' like they do in the House of Commons !"

Of this ill-timed pleasantry the attorney took no notice, his thoughts, to all appearance, being occupied with recollections of the past. The click of the decanters, however, as the rector passed them round, aroused him, and he helped himself to a bumper of sherry.

"That is to the governor," whispered John in my unwilling ear, "what 'God save the Queen' is to a band of music. When he has had his 'whitewash' he never drinks anything more."

And, indeed, within five minutes my uncle's old-fashioned inquiry of "Gentlemen, shall we join the ladies?" was answered by his chief guest in the affirmative, and we adjourned to the drawing-room.

As we entered it, my eye chanced first to fall upon Mrs. Raeburn; and though it was in search of someone else, the expression of her face arrested me. Her cold impassive features wore a strange look of anxiety upon

them, as she fixed her gaze upon her jovial-
looking husband.

"What folly have you been committing
now? what secret have you let out over
your cups?" it seemed to say.

In answer to which query the attorney's
flushed features had, to my fancy, a deprecating air. "There is nothing to be alarmed
at, my dear; but, I must confess, I have
been a little imprudent in my confidences,
and that's a fact."

I must have been highly imaginative
at that period of my life, for I distinctly
remember a horrible idea suggesting itself
to me out of that supposed dialogue between
man and wife. Was it possible, in years
to come, that Gertrude and I should ever
look at one another like that, or have the
same sordid hopes and fears in common?

The next moment I caught sight of my
darling, leaning over my aunt's blue sofa
cushion, like an angel on a cloud, and
endeavouring to grapple with the mysteries

of a new knitting stitch, which her hostess was teaching her.

" Here is Harry," whispered the old lady, slily, as I drew near them ; "you see, my dear, he wants to learn it too."

CHAPTER IV.

A REVELATION.

Our little dinner at the Rectory, though perfectly satisfactory in its material details, which, thanks to my aunt, were always perfect, could scarcely be said to be a success in a social point of view. It certainly did not bring the two families into closer connection with one another. At breakfast next morning my aunt pronounced Mrs. Raeburn to be a monstrosity, from which term, either in the way of mitigation or explanation, she was not to be moved an inch. As for John, she had read of such young persons in books, but had always thought them too hateful to have a real existence. While of Mr. Raeburn, she could only say in his favour that he was not a whit more vulgar than she had expected him to be. She allowed, however, in the men's case, that they were the victims of circumstances. "When Harry becomes an attorney, he will doubtless grow like the father, and if he had not gone to college"— this had always been a strong point with my aunt, and, indeed, it was to her views upon the matter that I owed my University career— "he would now be like the son. There must be attorneys"—this in answer to a mild observation of my uncle's to that effect —"quite true, my dear, though it is much to be regretted; and there must also always be young men who are not brought up at Oxford or Cambridge; but they have no business in society, and if they are found there, ought to be removed, or, at all events, avoided."

So she disposed of the whole family, and when I questioned her about Gertrude, she clashed her rings together with a little shriek of despair.

"My dear boy, don't speak of her. I couldn't help playing into your hands last evening, because I like to see young people happy, and the impulse of the moment over-powered me. She is charming, modest, beautiful—anything and everything you please; but there is an insuperable obstacle to my contemplating her as the future Mrs. Sheddon —you must dismiss her from your mind, once and for all, Harry."

"Why?"

"How can you ask me why? She is Mr. Raeburn's cousin, and if you suppose that I will ever submit to be connected with that family, you don't know your Aunt Eleanor."

My uncle's views respecting our guests were, as usual, of a much less decisive kind. Mrs. Raeburn was, indeed, he confessed, "a Gorgon"; "but what does it matter, my dear? There are two toll-gates between here and Kirkdale, and she will never call." As for the attorney, though the rector had had no intimacy with him for years—their business relations in the meantime, however, being continuous—he had known him when they were lads together, and was not inclined to pass any severe judgment on so old an acquaintance. "Whatever he is, he can deserve no worse than to have a wife like that. What a constitution she must have to be so strong and tough, when everything must turn acid with her." His good nature saw nothing particularly objectionable in John, whom indeed that escapade with the preserve cupboard had, I think, rather endeared to him. "He's a pleasant young fellow enough, if he wouldn't whistle at table."

"And what do you think, Ralph, of Miss Floyd?" asked my aunt, whose conversation with me upon that subject had occurred before my uncle had made his appearance at the breakfast-table.

"Well, 'pon my life," answered the

rector, laughing, "I think what Harry thinks. She has money too, you sly dog," added he, approvingly; "ten thousand pounds of her own, as Mark informed me, in a most unusual fit of confidence. I never saw him so communicative as he was last night. A strange story that he told about himself and his brother Alexander, was it not?"

"Very," observed my aunt contemptuously, to whom the narrative had doubtless been already communicated above stairs; "very strange if true; though to believe that your friend the attorney ever acted on an affectionate impulse is out of my power."

In spite of these unfavourable sentiments respecting the Raeburn family, the arrangements respecting my residing with them had of course to be carried out, and I migrated from Stanbrook to Kirkdale that very day.

My reception at the Priory was by no

means an enthusiastic one. Mrs. Raeburn
had, I fancy, been no better pleased with
her visit to the Rectory than her host and
hostess had been to see her there, for she
never even so much as asked after them;
while the attorney himself was far from
cordial. Either from the sense that my
premium was secure, and that there was
no further need to make himself agreeable,
or (which I think more probable) from the
consciousness of having somewhat committed
himself before me the previous evening, his
manner was reserved and formal; he wasted
no time in hospitable courtesies, but at once
proceeded to introduce me to my duties,
the sphere of which was of course his office.
This was a spacious apartment, built out
from the dining-room, and furnished with
two monstrous desks and one nondescript
article of furniture with curious legs, which
served the same purpose, though it more
resembled a pulpit. I had heard of persons
being "sold up" by the lawyers, and it

struck me that this might be the rostrum from which their goods were knocked down to the public.

"What is that?" inquired I.

"Why a desk, of course; John's desk: he likes it high."

The fact being, as I afterwards discovered, that it was an old "upright grand" piano, long past service, which Mrs. Raeburn had caused to assume this questionable shape, to avoid the necessity of procuring a new desk on my arrival. Many a time did John play on it, as though the keys had still been there to perform their office, choice airs of his own composing. Many a sermon did he preach from it, in imitation of the Rev. John Merrick, Vicar of Kirkdale; and many a time, in the character of the local auctioneer, did he dispose of the title-deeds of his father's clients to an imaginary audience, at exceedingly low figures. The walls were lined with shelves, on which reposed tin boxes, each containing some precious parchment, labelled without, Kirkdale-Manor Trust; Hawley Estate ; Lord Belcombe's Deeds, &c.

"Why, you have everybody in the county for your clients, Mr. Raeburn," said I.

"Well, pretty near all the good names, sir. There's your Uncle Ralph's, you see. His father, the late rector, did business with my father, and I hope his nephew and my son will be equally good friends. Yes, yes, for a mere local lawyer, he will have a tolerable practice, I flatter myself." The mention of my uncle's name seemed to have mellowed the attorney.

"What is that box with West Indies on it ?" asked I; "they are not in the county."

"Well, John calls it 'Hot Pickles,'" replied Mr. Raeburn, with a grim smile ; "for the fact is, it is rather a warm subject. There lie my wife's titles to her West India estates, which are no longer in existence. If you want to air your legal knowledge in this house, never choose the Emancipation Act as your topic. You are looking at Miss Floyd's box; and that reminds me that you rather 'put out' my wife last night, by your marked attention to Gertrude; and the poor girl caught it in consequence. Of course it was but natural on your part; but, in future, you must be more careful. Perhaps it will be better to let you know at once that she is engaged to John."

Here was a fiasco! Three hundred guineas paid out of my very moderate fortune, and three years' imprisonment before me in the Briary—besides the adoption of a profession for which, to say the least of it, I had no sort of liking—and all for nothing. If the attorney had taken down the large county map that hung over the fireplace, and knocked me down with the rollers, I could not have been more astonished nor more prostrated.

"Gertrude is my ward," he continued, "and my veto as to the disposal of her hand, while a minor, would have been absolute; but though they were cousins—which Mrs. Raeburn thought an objectionable circumstance—I had not the heart to refuse the young folks."

"Then their marriage is to take place immediately," observed I, with as much indifference as I could assume.

"Well, no, there is no hurry; some time within the next three years."

A gleam of hope illumined my inward gloom. Within three years her judgment would have matured, and she might change her mind. The idea of that lovely and graceful girl, who could appreciate true poetry, becoming the wife of John Raeburn, was too terrible to contemplate; but, then, what shocking contrasts matrimony did afford. The head of my college, a septuagenarian, had married a girl of seventeen, who had been the cynosure of all our eyes in chapel.

Mr. Raeburn's disclosure had taken me so utterly by surprise, for the moment, that I did not question its authenticity. Stunned and cast down, I listened with heedless ears to his details of my future office work and office hours; but when at last he had concluded them, and had shown me my own apartment, and left me there, and I sat down to contemplate my catastrophe at leisure, some uncertain lights broke in upon me.

It might, of course, have been the embarrassment of the topic itself that had caused him to avert his eyes from me while speaking of it; to play with the ruler; to use a tone of marked emphasis that contrasted strangely with his nervous manner; but it might also have been that he was not speaking the truth—or, at all events, speaking something more than the truth.

I could not credit, upon a review of what had passed between Gertrude and myself, that she was actually engaged to John Raeburn. No word of love, it is true, had been exchanged between us, or had, even on my part, been actually expressed; yet she could scarcely have been mistaken as to the nature of my attentions, and these she had undoubtedly encouraged. The thought that she had been playing into the attorney's hands, merely to ensure my becoming his articled clerk, flushed my cheek with shame for having entertained it even for an instant, and was dismissed at once and for ever. No; whatever arts had been used in that procedure, she at least was guiltless of them, though she might have been the innocent instrument of others. Perhaps Mr. Raeburn thought to pocket my three hundred guineas, and at the same time rid himself of an unwelcome pupil, by this unlooked-for revelation. In that case I would show him that I was tenacious of my rights, resolute to have my money's worth, and so far evidence a capacity for my new calling; I would not be starved out of my present quarters, though Mrs. Raeburn should diet me on home-made wine and periwinkles; and, above all, I would seek an early opportunity of hearing from Miss Floyd's own lips whether her guardian had told the truth or not.

In the drawing-room I found the whole family assembled, awaiting the announcement of dinner, which was at the Briary a movable feast, varying with the seasons; being in summer time at the fashionable hour of seven, in the autumn at six and five, and in the winter at three, the object of which complicated arrangement was to avoid the necessity and consequent expense of dining by candle-light. Miss Floyd rose to meet me with a quiet smile and the very faintest change of colour; if her manner was not absolutely cordial, it was as much so as, considering the presence in which we stood, it could have been expected to be; and when I pressed her hand, the pressure—and I watched for it as a doctor watches for a beat of pulse—was perceptibly returned. It might have been but as a sign of welcome, though even so I should have been thankful for it; but my heart,

which had been low and cold, leaped up at
that touch, like flame from ashes, taking it
as a more tender token. Her speech was
gentle as usual, but quite unembarrassed;
so that of one of two things I felt convinced—either Mrs. Raeburn had not rebuked her for my conduct of the previous
evening, in which case her husband had
told me an untruth, that had probably
been but one out of many; or if she had,
that it had had no effect upon her. Of the
two, I inclined to the latter opinion, for I
knew that Gertrude had a spirit of her
own that would resist unjustifiable censure,
while the fact of her pecuniary independence placed her out of the reach of absolute harshness. To her servants, to her
husband, to every one over whom she could
exercise supremacy, Mrs. Raeburn's manner
was dictatorial; to her equals, or those she
fancied to be her equals, it was morose and
taciturn; but to Gertrude she was always
patronisingly civil. She did not, indeed,

call her "Gerty," as John Raeburn did, but she termed her "cousin" — which, as a matter of fact, she was not—and in the morning and at night she applied that gash between her chin and nose to Miss Floyd's cheek (like a pike smelling at a water-lily) in motherly salutation.

It devolved on me, of course, to take Mrs. Raeburn into dinner, her husband followed with Gertrude, and behind came John, with a mincing gait, in supposed imitation of the ladies, that turned the servant girl in waiting purple with suppressed mirth. To my chagrin, I was placed by myself at Mrs. Raeburn's right hand, while Gertrude sat opposite with John. This, however, I reflected, was no less than what was to be expected from Mr. Raeburn's announcement, whether true or not; and certainly the young people did not conduct themselves, at least to my thinking, as engaged persons. If a single covert glance had been exchanged between them; if their hands had strayed together for one instant below the table-cloth; if, with a stolid glance at his father's picture on the wall, John had even ventured to press her fairy foot with his own—I should without doubt have been cognisant of it, so strict was my watch upon them; but none of these significant events occurred. They seemed on intimate terms indeed, but only such as might be looked for in the case of two young persons living under the same roof, and related—although, indeed, but distantly—to one another. Had I not already been acquainted with John Raeburn, his total freedom from embarrassment would have convinced me that there was " nothing between them;" but that symptom was in his case not to be depended upon. He would have been just as free and easy in his manners, if he had been accepted yesterday, or had been refused, or if he was going to marry his fair neighbour on the morrow.

Our dinner had one merit—it was not pretentious. There were two small soles, which, being set before my hostess, I offered to carve, a proposition which to my great satisfaction she declined. It required a mathematical genius to divide them into five portions, and yet leave a fragment on the dish. There was a boiled scrag-end of mutton, which was a dire cause of discomposure to me, since it naturally suggested caper sauce ; and when I asked for it, there was none. "Cook has forgotten it, I'm afraid," said my host, apologetically. "The cook has done nothing of the kind," was his wife's stern rejoinder. "In this house, Mr. Sheddon, though I trust you will find everything good and wholesome of its kind, you will find no luxuries. We avoid them upon principle. Some people, for instance, indulge in a profusion of foreign liquors ; now, in my opinion, the manufactures of our own country should be encouraged, rather than those of France or Spain ; so, although there is sherry, for those to whom a vicious custom has rendered it necessary"—here she

shot a rebukeful glance at the attorney—
" it is our usual custom to drink raisin or
ginger wine." Having had experience of the
sherry, my own opinion was that the charge
of foreign manufacture could scarcely be laid
against it; but, nevertheless, I took Mrs.
Raeburn's hint, and a glass of ginger wine.

Anything more objectionable I did not
remember to have put in my mouth since I
had been a school-boy; and I suppose the
expression of my countenance betrayed the
fact, for she added hastily, "It is a most
excellent stomachic."

At this, John Raeburn, who was in the
act of taking a dose of it himself, was seized
with an irresistible fit of laughter.

It was necessary, of course, to swallow
this admirable tonic remedy before its bene-
ficial attributes could take effect upon the
human system. In John's case, this pre-
liminary operation had not been completed,
and for some minutes I thought he would
have been choked.

"It went the wrong way," observed Mrs. Raeburn, either in explanation of this hideous catastrophe, or as an apology for her wine.

"If it went the right way," muttered the attorney, gloomily, "it should go into the hog-tub, every bottle of it."

The observation was a partially just one; but "By what an atmosphere," thought I, with indignation, "of vulgarity and meanness is yon angelic creature surrounded in this house!"

I felt like some heroic young seaman to whom a "cutting out" expedition has been for the first time entrusted; and from under the frowning battery of Mrs. Raeburn's guns I swore to myself to rescue the charming Gertrude, to haul down her cousin's colours (if indeed she wore them) from the mast, and to substitute in place of them my own. I was not so sanguine, or so venturous, as to think of asking her for the present whether I possessed her love; but I was resolved to know, that very evening, in what position she really stood with relation to John Raeburn, that I might shape my course accordingly.

CHAPTER V.

OUR sordid meal did not occupy much time; nor was there any great temptation to linger over the plate of biscuits—"mixed," said the hostess, but, in fact, consisting of five small abernethys and one infinitesimal macaroon—which, with some mystic preserve, the basis of which seemed to be damaged damsons, formed the dessert. After one more glass of ginger wine, to which she must have assimilated her constitution, for it never did her any hurt, Mrs. Raeburn thawed a smile at Gertrude, then froze again with dignity, and carried my charmer away with her into the drawing-room.

"John, bring the brandy," was the ejaculation uttered by the attorney, as the door closed upon his wife's majestic figure. "Your mother may call that wine of hers a stomachic, but I pronounce it stomach-ache. I am sure Sheddon must be suffering tortures."

John instantly dived into the office and produced a decanter of what looked like sherry, and of which his father insisted upon my partaking, under the transparent pretence that it had been sent for upon my account. The occurrence was evidently an habitual one, and when he had helped himself to a bumper, the host—for fear, as I concluded, of a sudden inroad from his better half—placed the bottle on the carpet beside his chair, as though it had been champagne in ice. Every hour that I had been at the Priory seemed to present some painful illustration of the character of one or other of its inmates.

My host was a drunkard, my hostess a screw,
John a clown, only Gertrude was tender and true,

was the verdict my experience passed upon my new acquaintances, and which my habit of verse-making cast into the above poetic form. I had plenty of leisure, both for reflection and composition, for Mr. Raeburn and his son began to talk over the business transactions of the day, which had no interest for me even when intelligible— how Farmer Dod had called about renewing his lease, and how Lord Belcombe's steward had objected; how Gaffer Gurdon's will, which he had insisted on making himself, would 'not prove very profitable to his niece, by the time the law had done with it; and how the superintendent of the borough police had been "squared" by the landlord of the "Dove with Two Heads."

Through the monotonous buzz of their talk, which, together with the effects of the unaccustomed glass of brandy, was fast lulling me to slumber, my ear suddenly caught the sound of wheels. The house stood quite apart by itself, with only a private road leading to it from the town, so that if any vehicle were coming that way it must needs be to the Priory. Any visitor would be welcome to me, as not only putting a stop to the present conversation, which seemed interminable, but as enabling me to escape to the drawing-room. I listened, however, to the rumble of the wheels upon the hard road, to the click of the entrance-gate ; and then to the craunch upon the gravel, with an interest that could scarcely have been warranted by such considerations. Years afterwards, when presentiments chanced to be the subject of talk, the unaccountable excitement I felt on the present occasion recurred to me, and made me silent instead of joining the side of the scoffers.

" I hear a gig," remarked John, presently.

" Nay," said I, to whom the sound was by this time quite familiar, " it is a four-wheeler of some sort."

" It is the brandy that makes you hear double," rejoined John, with his odious titter, which had this time a touch of malice in it, because, perhaps, his father had not offered him a glass. The old man knew too well the bitterness of the fruit of that tree of knowledge to offer it to his only son; and perhaps even foresaw a time wherein, even though he were yet alive, there should be but one head left to manage affairs the intricacy of which needed careful steering.

"It has passed the office door and is coming to the house. What a fool that little Jerry is! He is always making some mistake," said Mr. Raeburn, peevishly. "They should put some other man at the station."

"It isn't Jerry driving," answered John, who had risen, and was looking out of window. "It's a dog."

"A dog? You must be drunk, John!" exclaimed his father, rising also, but not without some difficulty.

As we all three stood at the window, we beheld this portent. A railway fly, with such an enormous bull-dog sitting on its front seat, that he absolutely concealed the driver (who was, however, but of very small dimensions) on the other side of him. Above the fly were some nondescript and shapeless articles of luggage, made of some wild animal's hide, with the hair outside (afterwards found to be a bison's). Within the fly, and looking out of its window, from which it nodded to us with an air of familiar recognition, was a very large scarlet bird, which, from the height at which it stood, might have been an ibis, but it had a parrot's beak.

"What the deuce is it?" murmured the attorney. There was positive apprehension in his tone, which in his case too might well have been presentiment, but which I believe to have been caused by the suspicion that his vision was playing him false; that the Nemesis of delirium tremens, of which he stood in fear, had already overtaken him.

"It's a menagerie," replied John, quietly.

"They think you are the mayor this year, instead of Wilmot, and are come to ask permission to exhibit in the Town Hall. There's the proprietor—that fellow with the white beard and the straw hat—and he has probably got a Bengal tiger under his seat."

The man alluded to had left the vehicle, and was standing at the front door, with the bird upon his wrist, like a falconer with a scarlet hawk, whilst the driver, evidently in abject terror of the bull-dog, was cautiously taking down the luggage.

"Who can it be?" reiterated the attorney, with a tremor in his voice even more perceptible than before.

"It is Robinson Crusoe, father," answered John, with imperturbable gravity. "His man Friday is to arrive by the next train, and they are come to stop with us over Christmas."

It was clear indeed that the visitor was not making an afternoon call, but intended to stay the night at all events. A considerable number of " effects " had been by this time taken out of the fly, and were accumulated about him : a large brass cage, probably the residence of the parrot ; two small deal boxes with slits in them, as though to hold money for some charitable institution ; two or three packages, looking like the offspring of the larger ones, and equally shapeless and hairy ; and an enormous umbrella.

" I thought so," ejaculated John, as this last article made its appearance ; " you will soon see his two guns and his tame goat."

But at that moment the front door opened, and the owner of all these wonderful properties disappeared within the house. There was a tumult of voices in the hall ; the chatter of the parrot, the growl of the dog, a shriek from the maid-servant, and presently the last-named came flying into the room with—

" Please, sir, a gentleman wants to see you."

"What about? What does he want?" inquired the attorney, who stuck fast by the window, looking very pale and embarrassed.

"I am sure I don't know, sir; he has a lot of birds, and beastesses, and serpents," added she, with terrified emphasis. "But missis has gone out to him."

It was plain that, in the maid's opinion, there was no man, nor beast, nor creeping thing, whom her mistress was not fully a match for; and yet we could now hear Mrs. Raeburn's voice, pitched many degrees lower than her usual tone.

"In that case, you had better see my husband at once, sir," she was saying, and the next moment the door opened and she entered, followed by the stranger and his myrmidons.

It looked like a segment of the procession into the ark, and yet John's simile of Crusoe held better than ever, for the parrot had left the stranger's wrist and was sitting upon his shoulder. He was a fine, handsome fellow, though his face, bronzed by a tropical sun, looked, by contrast with his long white beard, less like a copper kettle than the bottom of it after being exposed to the action of fire.

"Here's a gentleman who says he is your brother, Mr. Raeburn."

"Mark!" cried the stranger, opening his long arms, and looking earnestly at the attorney. "Dear Mark, don't you know me?"

Mr. Raeburn came hurriedly forward, and since the offer of his hand would evidently have fallen short of what was expected, yielded to his brother's embrace.

The ridiculousness of the scene was beyond description; for the attorney, quite unused to such a display of affection, was not only awkward in his accomplishment of it, but was evidently in mortal terror of the parrot, who, from his post on the stranger's vacant shoulder, emitted a series of discordant shrieks,

H 2

ending with, "Kiss and be friends! kiss and be friends! kiss and be friends!"

There was one thing, however, which, to my mind at least, rescued the proceeding from utter absurdity, and even invested it with pathos. The tall white-bearded man was shedding tears of joy.

"Thirty years ago, Mark; thirty years ago," reiterated he, in broken tones; "and yet that you should know me still!"

"I knew you, Alec," answered the other, not without corresponding tones of emotion, "when you first got out of the fly."

"Well, that is so far satisfactory," observed Mrs. Raeburn, who had been regarding these proceedings with considerable impatience and contempt; "because, really, nowadays, there is no knowing who's who."

"God bless you, Alec, and welcome home!" cried the attorney, hoarsely.

"Yes; welcome home to England," added Mrs. Raeburn, with some slight stress on the last two words. "You are come from abroad, of course ; and in health and prosperity, I hope. Mark has often and often talked about you."

The visitor turned his face towards his hostess with a questioning look ; then, after a little pause, exclaimed, " I do not doubt it, madam ; though, if I did, I should still thank you for saying so. When we were lads, we were all in all to one another. Now, of course, it is different. He has his wife—what's her name, Mark ? "

" Matilda."

" Let me salute you, Matilda." She stood like a graven image while her brother-in-law stepped up to her, parrot and all, and kissed her cheek ; though, from the expression of that bird's countenance, I should not have been a whit surprised had he pecked her eye out. " This is your eldest son ?

" Yes ; John," explained the attorney, absently, for the bull-dog was walking round and round his legs.

" And this your second ? " continued th

visitor, addressing me with the same genial smile that he had bestowed on my supposed brother. "Since your eldest son was not named after yourself, I can scarcely hope to find an Alexander in the family."

"He does not belong to the family at all," observed Mrs. Raeburn.

"I am sorry for it," answered the visitor, drily. "He looks a frank young fellow enough. I trust, however, I have at all events a relation in this charming young lady."

Gertrude had entered the dining-room, unobserved, in the confusion, and was standing close behind me.

"If you are Mr. Alexander Raeburn, my father, Robert Floyd, was your first cousin," answered she, sweetly. "I remember to have heard my mother speak of you," she added, with a little blush.

"Are you Maggie Warden's daughter?" exclaimed the bearded man, with a tremor in his manly voice. "I ought to have known as much. Would you mind if an old man like me should ask to kiss you?"

"That's nice! that's nice! that's nice!" shouted the parrot, as its master suited the action to the word. "Kiss and be friends! kiss and be friends! kiss and be friends!"

"I hope we shall, Chico; I am sure we shall," ejaculated the visitor, gravely. "God bless all in this house, and thanks be to Him that, after so many years, he has permitted me to come amongst them."

CHAPTER VI.

BROTHER ALEC.

THE explanation that I had promised myself
to obtain from Gertrude had, after all, to
be postponed, for it was impossible for any
of us to speak or think that evening, except
of " Brother Alec." He was by far the most
interesting and striking personage that had
come within the range of my small experience, and the effect he produced upon us all
was prodigious. Mrs. Raeburn, in particular,
entertained, or affected to entertain, a very
grave interest in her new-found brother-in-
law, though it was manifested with her usual
caution. She made no pretence to affection
for him; she could not even overcome her

niggardly disposition so much as to offer him refreshment.

"This room smells unpleasantly of dinner; had we not better go into the drawing-room?" was all the allusion she made to food: but she listened to him—especially when he spoke of his own fortunes—with rapt attention, and watched him like a cat at a mouse-hole.

As generally happens when a man returns to his own country, after long and distant travel, brother Alec's talk was at first confined to questioning those who had remained at home, and afterwards to his own later and English experiences—how he had fared at the hotel at Southampton; how the swiftness of the London express had astonished him; how the official had tried to compel his dog "Fury" to travel under the seat (which, however, a station-master and four aids had entirely failed to accomplish); and how his fellow-passengers had stared at his parrot, and laughed to hear it enter into

conversation. We were by no means astonished at these two last statements.

"Where did you get that dog from,
Uncle Alec?" was one of John's first inquiries.

"Ah, my pretty Fury!" returned the
other. This dog, by-the-way, was of a
super-canine ugliness. His immense weight
seemed to have bowed out his legs even
more than is customary with bull-dogs;
his head was very nearly of the same size
as his body; and he had no tail whatever,
but only a stump, which protruded in
such a manner that it needed most careful
adjustment before he could sit down. The
most remarkable feature, however, of this
attractive animal—I say attractive, because
it was impossible to withdraw your attention from him for a single instant, if he
happened to be in your neighbourhood—
was his eyes, which were fearfully blood-
shot, and seemed to resent the fact that
they had been fitted into inappropriate

sockets. They were not large eyes, whereas the sockets were very large, and the un- occupied portions of the rims were red and ragged, which heightened exceedingly the truculence of his general expression.

" My pretty Fury, yes ; he was the first thoroughly English face, as it were, that saluted me when I touched the land. His master was bound the next day for a foreign shore, as I found upon making acquaintance with him in the afternoon, and one of his chief regrets was that this dog could not be taken with him ; he had no friend that really loved the animal with whom he could leave him with confidence, and since it took a marvellous fancy to myself, he made me a present of it. For all its formidable looks, it would not hurt a child."

" That is not so much consequence to us," observed John, rather pertinently, " as that it will not hurt grown people."

" No, no, it will hurt nobody ; see how it already has taken to Miss Floyd yonder," observed its owner, "and is licking her hand," which indeed it was; and a more complete contrast of Beauty and Beast than the pair afforded it was impossible to imagine. "Fury is as harmless as Chico here."

Chico was the parrot, who, on hearing his name pronounced, pressed his scarlet head against his master's cheek and clawed his waistcoat lovingly, and, being answered with a finger of acknowledgment, took it

> " with all care,
> And bit it for true heart and not for harm."

"That is surely not a common parrot, Mr. Raeburn," observed Gertrude, admiringly.

"You are right, my dear young lady, though I must beg you to call me cousin, as you do my brother. It is a very uncommon parrot, as I have had to explain to everybody who has seen him. I do not believe there is another such a bird in

England. He is called the Night Talker, because all night long he makes conversation with himself, and is generally silent in the day, though my locomotive habits of late have put him out. The kind is rare even in the place from which I brought him ; which, by-the-by, I have not yet named. For these last five-and-twenty years, while you have thought me dead, Mark, my home has been in Peru."

"Peru!" exclaimed we all. It seemed so strange that he should speak of home in connection with so outlandish a country.

> "Let observation with extensive view
> Survey mankind from China to Peru,"

was the couplet that at once suggested itself to me. I had read but very little else about it.

"I have been living at Cuzco," he continued mildly, "which, as perhaps you may have heard, John, was the ancient residence of the Incas."

"Black people, are they not?" replied John, tentatively. He had a general notion that persons born out of Europe are black, and perhaps he thought Incas were spelt with a k.

"Indeed they are not," answered Uncle Alec, smiling. "They are of a beautiful bronze colour; at least the natives are, the upper classes being Spanish. I had thought, until an hour ago"—here he bowed with a certain quiet grace that made one forget his absurd surroundings altogether, and, notwithstanding his ill-fitting and hastily-made European garments, showed the true gentleman within them—"that no women in all the world could be compared with the Peruvians for loveliness."

"And is it possible, sir, that you should have lived among all these beauties for so many years," inquired Mrs. Raeburn, in a tone of raillery very foreign to her tongue, and which, as it seemed to me, was adopted in order to conceal the interest she felt in

the expected reply, "and yet remained un-
married ? "

"No, madam," answered Uncle Alec, with
grave frankness. "I was a bachelor for many
years ; the remembrance of one I had left in
England "—he kept his eyes fixed on Gertrude with such sorrowful tenderness that it
was easy to guess that he was alluding to
her mother—"was too strong to be easily
broken ; but in the end the present outwore
the absent, and I married."

"Did you have any children ?" inquired
Mrs. Raeburn. The whole topic, it was plain,
was painful to her brother-in-law ; but no
consideration of such a fact had the least influence with that indomitable woman.

"I had one baby boy, and when he died
his mother died with him," answered Uncle
Alec, in a voice that went to our very
hearts.

There was silence amongst us all, while
the tears stood in tender Gertrude's eyes,
and Mrs. Raeburn sighed—a very satisfac-

tory sort of sigh indeed. I had not forgotten
her husband's revelation at the rector's table,
of the facts of which she had doubtless long
been cognisant, and by that light it was not
difficult to read to what end her questions
had been put. If Uncle Alec were poor, I
knew her well enough to feel convinced that
he would find himself no better off by reason
of the solemn covenant made with her husband
thirty years ago ; but if he were rich, and
without encumbrance in the shape of wife or
child, it would be worth her while to conciliate
this man—frank, impulsive, simple-hearted, as
he seemed to be—to the uttermost. Mark,
on the other hand, had asked no questions
of his brother, but, with his eyes fixed con-
stantly upon him, had stood with his chin
in his hand, his usual attitude when in
thought.

He was now, however, the first to break
silence.

"You have never told us, Alec, how it
was that for all these many, many years we

have heard nothing from you, and had learnt to think you dead. How was it ?"

"That is a question hard to answer, Mark ; having to go so far back in my mind for the materials of the reply. It was something of this sort, I think, however. When we two last parted at Southampton —you have not forgotten that occasion, Mark ?"

"I have not, brother," answered the attorney, a slight flush rising to his face, which had been deadly pale.

"When we parted then, you remember how light and buoyant were my spirits ; how sanguine I felt of coming back in a few years, with a fortune reaped beyond the Atlantic ; how confident I was in my youth, and strength, and wits. Well, not only did I reap no harvest in the field I had selected, but I lost there the few grains—you know how few they were, for you had the like— which I had gleaned at home. You said it would be so ; you advised my staying here

in England, and showed how, standing shoulder to shoulder (as we should have stood,
Heaven knows), that we might have pushed
our way in the Old World ; and because your
warning had been justified, and because I
had a devil of pride within me, I could not
bring myself to confess the truth—that you
were right, and I had been over sanguine.
If I succeeded, I said, then I will go back
to Mark, with both hands full of gold, and
one hand full for him——"

"One moment, my dear sir," interrupted
Mrs. Raeburn, with a smile almost as wide
as the bull-dog's ; "entranced by your interesting talk, and overcome by the emotions
natural to the occasion, I have, up to this
moment, wholly forgotten that you are not
only our brother, but our guest; your journey has been a long one, and you have
doubtless much to tell. Do let me offer you
some sherry and a biscuit, until something
more substantial can be got ready."

"Thank you, dear madam, I have already

dined," answered Uncle Alec, courteously; "but if you would be kind enough to get something for Fury, here; he likes a beef-steak, underdone, better than anything; and a little something hot for my serpents——"

"Your servants!" ejaculated Mrs. Rae-burn, with an involuntary groan. "I did not know you had brought any."

"Nor have I, dear madam" (I noticed he never called her "Matilda" after that first time); "though, in one sense, my serpents are my servants, since they do what-ever I bid them. In those flat boxes, left in the hall, there are a couple of diminutive anacondas, who have been my companions throughout the voyage, and indeed, have occupied the same berth. They are perfectly harmless, and require nothing but warm bread and milk, with an occasional rabbit."

"He means Welsh rabbit—toasted cheese," whispered John, in my ear. "As for his parrot, it requires human flesh, and will begin with my mother's cheek."

That remarkable bird, indeed, evidently regarded our hostess with no favour, and was craning towards her from its master's shoulder, with open beak and ruffled plumes, in a highly cannibalish way.

"Soft, Chico, soft," said Uncle Alec, rebukefully; "if you happen to have a cocoanut in the house, dear madam—but no, that is not likely: a fine fig then, or even an orange, will suit him admirably."

"I will get an orange for him, and see to the other things, Mrs. Raeburn, if you will give me the keys," observed Gertrude, "so that you need not leave cousin Alec."

Our visitor cast on her a grateful look, doubtless more in acknowledgment of her having used that title, than of her readiness to supply the wants of his favourites, about which there probably seemed to him no sort of difficulty. But Mrs. Raeburn's countenance was a study. The idea of giving beefsteaks to the dog, bread and milk to the serpents, and a fine fig to her declared enemy, the parrot, was almost intolerable : yet the thought of that "handful of gold," that was to have been, and perhaps still was, for Mark, overcame her repugnance, and with a muffled groan she surrendered the keys.

"Well, Mark," continued his brother, "I made up my mind, as I was saying, to send you no news of me unless it was good news ; and, alas ! the 'good' was years and years in coming to me ; so long that I grew ashamed, and almost afraid of writing at all. It is a lame excuse, I feel. But you don't know—I thank Heaven you have never known—what a change can come over a proud spirit, bent beneath the yoke of almost unremunerated toil, bowed by degrading servitude, crushed by the pitiless feet of those whom it would fain have despised. You who are rich, respected, and surrounded by those near and dear to you, cannot understand what happens to a lonely, friendless, poverty-stricken creature, such as I was ; how hope dies out within him, and the bitterness of

despair enters in instead, and turns his blood
to gall.   I loved you, Mark, at all times, even
at my worst, but it was a different sort of
love than that of old; there seemed a gulf
between us, and as I was changed, I knew,
so I thought might you have been.   If I
had the means to have come back, haggard
and ragged as I was, I should not have dared
to do it, lest my welcome might have been
cold, dear Mark, and all that was human in
me still should have been frozen by it.   I
did you wrong, you would say," added the
speaker hastily, laying his hand upon the
other's shoulder; "I know it, nay, I knew
it then.   Forgive me, and forget it."

It is impossible to reproduce the tender
earnestness with which these words were
uttered.   The attorney's face showed signs of
an answering emotion, though a certain hesi-
tation seemed to mix with it that made it
very different from that of his brother.   Even
"my son John" forbore to utter his ill-timed
pleasantries ; and Mrs. Raeburn kept a silenc

which was really creditable to her in the eyes of those who knew how strongly tempted she must have been to express contempt.

"And when was it, cousin Alec," inquired Gertrude, softly, "that your fortunes began to mend?"

"Thanks, Gertrude, thanks," said the old man. "I am grateful to you for cutting short the recollection of a grievous time — of such dark and weary years that they cast back their shadow even on this happy present. My luck did change at last. A southern gentleman, whom I had the good fortune to rescue from some unpleasant customers in New York one night, became my friend. It was perhaps sent for a reproof to me, Mark, that the talents on which I had reckoned so proudly to win my way in the world were fated to go for nothing, while my mere thews and sinews placed me on the first round of the ladder of prosperity. This gentleman, who had a great estate, and was a politician of some mark in his own country, made me his secretary, treated me in every respect as his equal—for which I felt more grateful to him than for all besides—and took me with him to New Orleans. I felt another man there ; recovered my self-respect, and found, to my great joy, that I could make myself useful to my benefactor, Mr. Pittsburg. My salary was liberal, and, thanks to him, I was introduced into good society, and began once more to hold my head up in the world.

"It was a life not only new to me, but one that would have seemed strange to any Englishman. Among the rich were the greatest luxury and idleness ; no literature, no arts ; no business was ever transacted among them ; splendid hospitalities, diversified by quarrels and duels, alone occupied their time. There was a young man of my own age, a planter, named Redman, who was said to have killed a dozen men with his unerring pistol, and who was greatly

respected in consequence. His estate bor-
dered upon that of Mr. Pittsburg, and he
was a constant, though, I fancied, not a
very welcome, visitor at his house. Mr.
Pittsburg had a son, a mere stripling, whom
he passionately loved, and for whose sake
I soon found out that he kept on friendly
terms with Redman, lest he should pick a
quarrel with the lad, and add him to his
numerous victims. For this reason, I have
no doubt, it was that when this Redman
behaved himself very contemptuously towards
myself—taking advantage, as no other man
did, of my dependent position—my patron
besought me not to resent it. I obeyed him.
I protest that that scoundrel's insults to me
were comparatively unfelt, so much more
did I burn to avenge the social oppression
which he exercised over my benefactor and
his family. He was by nature a tyrant, and
his cruelty to his numerous slaves was,
even in that country, where a black skin
is held of such small account, spoken of,

though with bated breath, with reprobation and disgust."

" By persons who had no slaves to deal with, I conclude," observed Mrs. Raeburn, coldly.

" Nay," answered brother Alec, surprised at this unlooked-for interruption, " by everybody. Indeed, there were, unhappily, but very few persons in Richmond who had no slaves to deal with."

Mrs. Raeburn concentrated her outraged feelings into one sniff of contemptuous defiance, and the interjection " Oh !" whereupon her relative resumed his story.

" I had been nearly twelve months at Rosemount, as Mr. Pittsburg's country house was called, when, walking one morning in the grounds alone, my ears were pierced by the most appalling cries of ' Help ' and ' Mercy.' Running in the direction from which the sounds proceeded, I found myself the spectator of a frightful scene. A negro girl lay stretched upon the ground, while

two white men stood over her, one of whom
was applying a cowhide to her naked flesh.
I had seen black men beaten often, but this
was the first time that I had ever beheld
such punishment inflicted upon a woman. My
blood boiled within me, and, without thinking of consequences, I rushed between the
torturer and his victim, and confronted him
with an indignant, 'Stop, you coward!'
I thought that it was some overlooker of
my patron who was thus indulging his
brutality, in defiance of his master's orders,
for, though by no means what we term a
'sentimental' man, Mr. Pittsburg always
opposed himself to harshness in the treatment of his black people. To my intense
astonishment (for I thought that I stood
on Mr. Pittsburg's land), I found myself
opposite Hugh Redman. For the moment
he was abashed at my discovering him in
the commission of an act which, even among
the harshest masters, was usually delegated
o their subordinates only.

"'Are you aware that this is my plantation?' inquired the ruffian, with his whip still raised over his shoulder.

"'I care not,' said I, 'whose plantation it is. To whip a girl like that is a disgrace to any human being, and an insult to the God who made her.'

"'We do what we like with our own here, Mister,' replied Redman, with a contemptuous laugh, 'and you had better get out of my way, or you will taste the cowhide yourself.'

"'The girl was skulking work,' explained the overseer, who stood behind his master, in an apologetic tone. He knew the tales that were told about 'Hell Gates,' as the plantation was termed, from the sufferings of its hands, and did not desire that a new witness to the appropriateness of that title should be added in my person.

"'What is that to him?' continued Redman, passionately. 'I shall whip whom I please, without excusing myself to any soul alive, far less to an upstart hanger-on like this fellow, who has nothing white about him except his liver.'

"I well understood this taunt to refer to the patience with which I had so long submitted to this ruffian's insolence, and which he naturally enough attributed to my cowardice ; but, furious as it made me, I take Heaven to witness that it raised not half the fury which consumed me when he once more brought down the sounding lash upon that poor defenceless creature. Her cry to him for mercy, to God for death to relieve her from such frightful torture, still rings in my ears. In an instant I had snatched the whip from the scoundrel's hand, and laid it over his face with such good-will that the blood spurted from his cheeks, as it had done from his victim's naked limbs. The overseer, who had sprang upon me in aid of his master, I saluted with the butt-end, which, as it happened, was heavily weighted, and it felled him insensible to the

ground.   Hugh Redman was not a brave
man—how could so base a wretch be brave?
—unless he had a pistol in his hand, his
skill in which gave him so deadly an advantage over his fellows ; and with a shriek
of rage and pain he fled from my second
blow, with his hand clapped to his dis-
figured face.   I was left alone with the tortured girl, who had crept towards me, as
a protector sent from Heaven itself, and
was embracing my knees.

"'Poor soul, what is to be done with
you?' was the involuntary exclamation that
escaped me.

"'Never mind poor nigger girl,' was her
piteous moan; 'she is used to be whipped.
Get away, or massa will come with pistol
and kill you.'

"'That is very likely,' thought I; but I
endeavoured to comfort her all I could.   I
felt no doubt that when Redman had called
me out and shot me—which it would be his
immediate business to do — this poor girl

would become the only object left on which
to wreak his vengeance; my interference
would, in fact, so far from doing her service,
be the cause of untold wretchedness to her;
so, therefore, it was only right that I should,
if possible, secure her safety. I gave her
what money I had about me, and certain
instructions, which, if carried out — though
it must needs be at great risk—would put
her into communication with some friends
of mine, who were connected with the
'Underground Railway,' the system by which
runaway slaves were helped by abolitionists
to the land of liberty. She was to make
no attempt in the matter until after the
result of the duel, which I felt sure was
inevitable. If I fell, she was to fly; and
if—though of that indeed there was but a
slender chance—I should kill my adversary,
I would get my patron to purchase the girl's
freedom.

"When I reached home and told Mr.
Pittsburg what had taken place, he looked

grave indeed ; I well knew what was passing through his mind, and pitied him from the bottom of my heart. Hugh Redman would not be satisfied with one victim in reparation for the insult that had been put upon him ; his hatred would extend to those who had harboured and been friendly to the man that had slashed his sneering face for him, and he would seek his quarrel with him who was far dearer to my host than his own life— namely, his only son. My heart bled for my kind friend ; and yet I could not wish that night's work undone, nor that I had held my hand when that poor slave had invoked its aid.

" ' Raeburn,' said Mr. Pittsburg, after a long silence, during which he had been pacing thoughtfully up and down the room, ' you must shoot this scoundrel, and I will teach you how to do it. You have no experience with the pistol, I believe ? '

" ' None whatever.'

" So much the better, you will have nothing

to unlearn. You have a keen eye and good nerves, I know; can you measure distances? Well, no matter — we shall have time for practice, if you have marked Redman as severely as you say. The dainty gentleman will not come out to fight till his wounds have healed, I'll answer for it.'

" I had long known that my enemy was no favourite with Mr. Pittsburg, but I had no idea how cordially he hated him, till I heard him say those words. From that moment he devoted himself to preparing me for the approaching conflict, and though I understood the intention of but half his teaching, I set myself diligently to acquire all he would have me learn. A billiard-room of very large proportions was built on one side of Rosemount, and out of this he caused the table and other furniture to be taken, in order to use it as a shooting-gallery; but that very night, and before I took pistol in hand, he set me to judge my distances, bidding me stop short when I considered that I

had approached a certain object within four-
and-twenty feet. In the billiard-room, but
mostly out of doors, I practised this un-
ceasingly, so that at last I was never wrong,
beyond a few inches. In the meantime —
indeed on the very morning after his cow-
hiding—Redman sent me a challenge, and
a meeting was appointed for ten days hence,
the unusual length of time being my adversary's own stipulation, upon the plea that
his eyesight had been injured in our recent
'conflict,' as he termed it. The interval,
however, was of immense advantage to myself.

" On the outer wall of the billiard-room,
Mr. Pittsburg sketched out a human figure,
of about the size and bulk of my future
opponent, and at this I practised with the
pistol for many hours a day ; walking slowly
from the other end of the room, and then
discharging the weapon when I had come
exactly within twenty-four feet of the object.
By incessant application, aided by a keen
eye and a steady hand, I had learnt, before

the appointed ten days had elapsed, to hit
an imaginary spot on the waistcoat of the
figure (exactly over its breast) three times
out of every four, nor was the fourth shot
very wide of the mark.   But while acknow-
ledging my progress, my tutor was well
aware that firing at a fixed object was a
very different matter from firing at an ad-
vancing one, especially when the latter had
a loaded pistol in his hand wherewith to
return the compliment; and I went on per-
fecting my aim as much as possible, even
to the very morning of the duel.   Mr. Pittsburg himself accompanied me to the place
of meeting as my second.

" 'This Redman will endeavour to frighten
you,' said he, ' by his boastful talk and also
by his ugly looks, which the whipping you
gave him has, I hear, not improved; but
pay no heed to him.   You will be arranged
one hundred feet apart, and when the handkerchief is dropped you will advance upon
each other, pistol in hand, firing when you

please. It is this man's invariable custom
to reserve his bullet until he comes within
twenty feet, at which distance he can split
a pea. When he comes within twenty-four
feet, therefore, be sure to fire; it is your
only chance of life.'

"Just as my patron had predicted, Redman came upon the ground, talking loudly
to his friends—of whom he had several with
him—and taking care to let me hear at
what hotel in the city he was to dine that
day after our affair was over. A livid seam,
which ten days of cold applications had not
erased, crossed his grim cheek and made him
horrible to behold, as he cast his cruel eyes
upon me.

"When the handkerchief was dropped he
did not, as I expected, cover me with his
pistol, but held it loosely downwards, while
he advanced with a menacing air, slightly
swaying his arms. At twenty feet from his
victims it was his habit to become suddenly
rigid, and to discharge his weapon as from

a fixed battery. My heart beat fast, as I beheld him thus approaching, but I did not omit to calculate my four-and-twenty feet; and when, as I judged, that exact distance lay between us, I fired and shot him dead."

"Bless my soul!" ejaculated the attorney; "why, by the twentieth of Charles, 1670, that was murder."

"Not in Richmond county, however," answered brother Alec, gravely; "nor, as I humbly hope, in the statutes of Heaven. For my part, I had no more compunction in killing such a wretch than I should have felt in slaying any other ferocious wild beast that is a terror to men and women. The thought of that tortured girl, and of the miseries that would have been in store for her, had my aim been unsuccessful, nerved hand and eye, as I covered him with my weapon, and I felt as though I were my-self an instrument in the hand of avenging Heaven. Everybody congratulated me (and himself) upon the result of the encounter; yet, strange to say, when it leaked out that the quarrel had taken place about a negro slave, public opinion turned against me, and it became absolutely impossible for me to continue at Richmond."

"That is generally the result of the enterprises of knight-errants nowadays," observed Mrs. Raeburn.

"At least, dear madam, there was nothing Quixotic in my conduct, I hope," returned brother Alec mildly. "I only did what your husband, your son, or this young gentleman here, would surely also have done in protecting a woman from most infamous and degrading treatment."

"A black woman, however," answered she, contemptuously. "What does the Scripture say concerning bondsmen: 'He shall be brought unto the doorpost, and his master shall bore his ear through with an awl; and he shall serve him for ever.' People will never persuade me, no matter how they cant and whine, that black folks feel as we do."

" That is a very soothing argument for whites, madam ; but suppose you had been born black yourself ? "

To look at Mrs. Raeburn at that moment, you would have thought she had been born so, and had kept her colour particularly well. She was naturally swarthy, and the thundercloud which formed upon her brow at this rejoinder, in spite of all considerations of prudence, would have raised the " drum " at any meteorological station. She answered not a word ; but all of us, save the new comer himself, were aware that, from that moment, Alec Raeburn had made an enemy for life in the woman he had chosen for his hostess. Though ignorant of the full extent of his *fiasco*, our Ulysses perceived that he had given offence, and, on the plea of being used to early hours, desisted for that time from narrating his adventures, and asked permission to retire for the night. The attorney accompanied his brother to his apartment, but leaving Mrs. Raeburn in the drawing-room, before whom it was impossible to discuss the new arrival, so we presently followed his example and went to bed.

The last thing I remember before I went to sleep was, my door being cautiously opened, and a voice, half suffocated with laughter, repeating the words, "Divide, divide, divide!" in parrot-like tones, as though Chico had been elected a member of the British senate.

CHAPTER VII.

A NIGHT ALARM.

THERE was nothing at this time of my life, save, now and then, some blissful castle-building in relation to Gertrude, which ever robbed me of my sleep, and yet, on the night which followed "Brother Alec's" arrival at the Priory, I scarcely closed my eyes. That far-travelled man, with his strange equipment and weird belongings, interested me beyond measure; and I found myself endeavouring to picture him when he was a lad of my own age—sanguine and impulsive—and then to follow him through the various phases of his character, as experience evolved or moulded them, until I arrived at what he had eventually become. In this last attempt, however, I felt myself baffled. That he was as simple and sensitive as a child, was clear enough; but I was not so sure that his wild career had not left its mark upon his character. Patient and conciliatory as he had shown himself to Mrs. Raeburn, it had seemed to me, who had watched him narrowly, that his forbearance had cost him a severe effort; when she spoke of slavery, in particular, there had been a slumbering fire of indignation in his eye suggestive of a hidden volcano. He appeared to me to have comprehended the whole situation, so far as his sister-in-law was concerned; how that she was the ruling power in the house, and the one to whom he must look for aid—if aid he needed—since his brother, with all the goodwill in the world to help him, could only do so by her permission; and knowing this, I fancied he resented it. If poor, her treatment of him, though intended to be prudently polite, must have been sufficiently galling; if rich, he probably regarded her—except upon his brother's account, to whom it was certain he was tenderly attached at present, however future experience might dispel his illusions—with contemptuous indifference. I would have given much, though I dare say not so much as my thrifty hostess would have given, to know in which of these two characters Alec Raeburn had returned to his native land; whether as an expectant sharer of his brother's bounty, or as the intending donor of half a splendid fortune.

It never crossed my mind that he had forgotten the agreement of thirty years ago, or would ignore it, or would look upon it as having anything less than the full force of law; and this certainly I gathered, not alone from his own tone and manner— which, though he had made not the faintest allusion to such an arrangement, seemed to me to take it for granted—but from the behaviour of the attorney himself. In Mark

Racburn all the tender feeling which years
and the practice of his profession had left
in him, had been stirred, it was easy to see,
to the very depths, by the arrival of his
once-beloved brother; and yet it was as
evident that it had overwhelmed him with
apprehension and dismay. I could not help
calling to mind the state of things mirrored
by the poet:

> " That could the dead, whose dying eyes
>   Were closed with wail, resume their life,
>   They would but find in child and wife
> An iron welcome when they rise."

For was not this man risen, as it were,
from the dead — from a grave of thirty
years—and vainly looking for the affection
which had been lavished on him at the
moment of his departure? To expect the
chain of Love to hold when so many links
were missing was to be over-sanguine, but
to look for it to run on as before, without
even showing where the break had been,

was to cast anchor in the sand. A few days, or weeks at farthest, must needs show the futility of such a hope, unless, indeed, Interest should step in and forge such links as might be mistaken by a fond and willing mind for the true metal. Perchance it would do so; perhaps in one of those uncouth portmanteaus might be scrip and share enough —or even bullion; for here was just the man to carry wealth about with him in the most tangible form—to make Brother Alec welcome to live on at the Priory; and, still more, to die there, leaving his wealth behind him.

Here, picturing bars of gold and rouleaux of dollars, I dozed off, to be awakened by a series of such hideous screams as had never before saluted my ear. They were inarticulate, yet seemed to appeal to Heaven and earth against murder "most foul and most unnatural." They came from the "spare room" next to mine, and in which "Brother Alec" had been put. "Was it possible," thought I, still half asleep, "that on the very first night beneath his kinsman's roof this trustful guest should have his throat cut for his gold?" Leaping from my bed, I rushed into the passage only to rush back again for my dressing-gown, for around my neighbour's door there was already a little crowd collected, including Mrs. Raeburn herself. I remember well, in that moment of horror, that it was quite a comfort to me to reflect that she, at all events, could not have committed the crime which seemed even now in course of accomplishment.

"What is the matter?" cried the attorney, beating frantically at his brother's door, which defied his attempts to open it, while the screams shrilled through our ears with the force and vehemence of a railway whistle.

"Eh, eh, hullo!" returned a voice, much dulled with slumber. There was a yawn, and a stumble on the floor, and then the door was opened, revealing the figure of our visitor in a sort of West Indian costume, in which it appeared he slept, like that of a journeyman baker, and vigorously rubbing his eyes. "What is it, Mark?"

"My dear Alec, that is what we ask of you? Are you ill? Are you mad? What nightmare can have made you yell like that?"

"I had no nightmare; I never opened my mouth, that I am aware of!"

"Time to get up! time to get up! time to get up!" ejaculated a discordant voice behind him; and on the mantelpiece, perched on the clock, which pointed to a little past three o'clock, stood the scarlet parrot.

"Oh, it's only Chico!" observed Brother Alec, mildly. "He never disturbs me; but when the clock strikes during the small hours, he often indulges himself in a 'View holloa.' That is why he is called the Night Talker. They didn't like it on board the ship at first, but they soon got used to it."

"Used to it!" exclaimed Mrs. Raeburn, indignantly. "Why, who *could* get used to it? It is lucky we don't live in the town, or that bird would have called the police."

"He does that sometimes, madam," answered our imperturbable visitor. "Call the police, Chico."

"Po—leese! po—leese! po—leese!" cried the parrot, thus invited, and shrieking at the full pitch of his voice. Then, very rapidly, "P'leese! p'leese! p'leese! p'leese! p'leese!" with which, as though to signify that the performance was quite concluded, he fluttered down upon the hearthrug and placed his head underneath his wing.

"Now he will be quiet for the rest of the night," observed his master, confidently, "unless," added he, "by any accident, one of the snakes should crawl over him. The naughty bird shall apologise in the morning for having disturbed you all."

"One moment!" exclaimed Mrs. Raeburn, with lifted finger—tall and gaunt, and wrapped up in her chintz dressing-gown, she might easily have been taken for a Wizard, though certainly not for an Enchantress—"this untimely disturbance may, after all, have been sent for our good, Mark. I smell fire!"

The attorney sniffed, as in duty bound.

"My dear," said he, "I only smell smoke."

"Smoke and fire are much the same things, I believe," replied she sternly. "If this sort of thing is to be permitted, we shall all be burned in our beds."

"Is it possible you allude to my tobacco, dear madam?" inquired Brother Alec, innocently. "It is true that, for many years, it has been my custom to smoke in bed; but, if you are nervous about the consequences, I promise you it shall not occur again. I will in future always take my pipe by the fireplace. I shall get used to all your English ways in time, no doubt, and become perfectly civilised."

Here he nodded pleasantly to us, and

closed the door, so that the expression of disgust and incredulity which Mrs. Raeburn's countenance displayed was, unhappily, lost upon him.

"This is positively unbearable," cried she, "to know that he will continue to smoke in his bedroom——"

"Hush, hush!" said the attorney, softly; "we must allow for foreign habits."

Mrs. Raeburn's countenance was by no means expressive of charity either to natives or foreigners; but, nevertheless, she suffered herself to be led back to her room.

No sooner had she disappeared than her hopeful son, who, in an airy costume at his own door, had been manifesting, by pantomimic action, his extreme delight at the whole proceedings, executed a noiseless harlequinade which landed him in my apartment.

"Did you ever see such a jolly go?" cried he, in a hushed rapture. "Did you ever hear such a love of a bird?"

"I must say," assented I, "that the whole affair is exceedingly comical."

"Comical! my dear fellow. If you only knew what I know, you would say it was excruciatingly funny. I have had to stuff my handkerchief in my mouth for the last two hours, even before that bird began, lest I should explode with laughter. It would be very wrong to talk of such matters, if my father had not himself let out the secret over your uncle's port-wine the other night; but as it is, there can be no great harm in telling you how my estimable parents are nonplussed by the new arrival. I can't keep it to myself, at all events," added he, apologetically; "I can't, indeed. Is Uncle Alec a Dives, or is he a Lazarus, is the question upon which a family conclave has been sitting for half the night."

"'If he is not rich, Mark' (and here Mr. John Raeburn imitated the air and tone of his maternal parent to the life), 'it is not possible that he would have dared to come here uninvited, with dogs, and birds, and serpents. That would be beyond the utmost stretch of human impudence.'

"Then my father" (though it was quite unnecessary for the histrionic John to say *that*) : "'Well, I'm sure I don't know, my dear Matilda. Alec was always a very cool hand—very.'

"'Cool, Mark! If that man is poor, he ought to be hung. Beefsteaks for his bull-dog, oranges for his parrot, bread-and-milk for his serpents—no, no; he must be very, very rich, that's certain.'

"'Let us hope so, my dear.'

"'And I can see this, Mark, that he takes a great interest in the family : the like-ness of our John to himself, which—except for that ridiculous beard, which makes him look like a savage—is most remarkable, and cannot but be very gratifying to him. Yes; he must dismiss his menagerie, and dress and shave himself like a Christian. It is your duty, as his brother, to tell him that; and then I am sure I shall grudge no pains nor trouble to make him comfortable. His ideas, indeed, are shocking, and subversive of all authority; but he has hitherto been exposed to no religious influences; as how should he be, living in such uncivilised parts? But we must not forget that he is your own flesh and blood. I think you were quite right not to ask him point-blank whether he had made his fortune. He will, doubtless, himself, acquaint us with that fact, and then it will be time enough to recall to his mind the little agreement which you made with him at parting. When a man comes from Peru, he is not likely to have merely secured a competence. We must give a dinner-party or two, to introduce him to our neighbours, and it will be quite as well to let them know what a millionaire he is.'

"'When we know it ourselves, my dear,

by all means ; but I don't think we should
be too precipitate. Alec always held that
there could be no obligation on either side
between him and me ; and it is just possible
—mind, I do not say it is so—but it is
just possible, that he may have come home
here, without a penny in his pocket, count-
ing upon the hospitality which, were our
cases reversed, he would certainly not refuse
to me.'

" To see my maternal parent's face,
Sheddon, when my father delivered himself
of that suspicion, was many degrees better
than a play.

" 'Mark,' says she, 'I sometimes think
that it is possible for a man to be a very
clever attorney, and yet to be a fool.' But
still it was plain that my mother could not
dismiss the notion from her mind that the
governor might be right ; and when that
parrot broke out just now, and Uncle Alec
confessed to smoking in bed, the thought

that he *was* right, brought, I could see, matters to within that much" (here John portioned off the extreme tip of his finger-nail) " of a Tremendous Explosion ; and to see poor Uncle Alec, so unconscious, and so polite, in his Peruvian uniform, too, and with that awful dog blinking round the corner, and all at three o'clock in the morning—oh dear! oh dear! oh dear!"

So hearty was my companion's burst of merriment, that I could not, for the life of me, help joining in it, though I felt how wrong it was in him to make a jest of the family anxieties, and especially of his mother. To remonstrate, however, with a born joker, such as John, and one, too, so absolutely devoid of delicacy of feeling, would have been mere waste of breath ; moreover, I was young myself, and to a joke at Mrs. Raeburn's expense I could be hardly expected to refuse a welcome.

At the same time (so convenient are the

arguments of self-interest) I reflected that this was but another proof, if one were needed, of the vulgarity of John's character, and of his total unfitness to aspire to the hand of Gertrude Floyd.

CHAPTER VIII.

IN THE GARDEN.

WHEN Uncle Alec came down to breakfast next morning, in company with his dog, the storm had blown over from Mrs. Raeburn's brow, and she received him with urbanity. The table at the Priory was not well provided at any meal, and especially at the earliest one ; but what delicacies there were —some rashers of bacon, a cold cutlet, which advanced age had tinged with grey, and a magnificent pot of home-made marmalade— were pressed upon him ; nay, he was even asked if he would like to have an egg. These proffers of hospitality he received so much as a matter of course, that a triumphant glance shot more than once from our hostess to her husband : "It is impossible" (it seemed to say) "that my conviction should not be correct; this man has all the ease in accepting favours which belongs to one who has the power of returning them."

When Mrs. Raeburn suggested that he might find the anacondas an incumbrance, and even suggested his offering them to the Zoological Society in London, who would doubtless elect him a Fellow in return for that donation, he did not take the hint with precipitation.

"Well, I'll think about that, my dear madam; the pretty creatures and myself have a great attachment to one another, and we should be loath to part. If you had little children in the house, I am sure I should have their voices in favour of retaining them, for gentler playmates it is impossible to imagine. To see them swarm up the banisters of a staircase—like the living tendrils of a vine—is one of the prettiest sights in nature; the elder one follows me like a dog."

"Are you going to take him with you into Kirkdale this morning, Uncle Alec?" inquired John, demurely.

"No, my boy, no. The fact is, it would be a dangerous thing to do in England."

"I should think it would!" ejaculated Mrs. Raeburn.

"Yes, madam, on account of the pigs," continued Uncle Alec, imperturbably. "Though men and boys would think twice before interfering with my spotted favourites, a pig would snap them up, and destroy them in an instant."

"You don't say so," said Mrs. Raeburn, with an air of much relief. It was evident that the question as to whether it is better to grow one's own pork, or to buy it, was settled from that moment in her own mind. She had resolved to keep a pig.

"After all," pursued Brother Alec, "anacondas, though not indeed such docile specimens as I have above stairs, are common enough. The Zoological Society have plenty of them, and can easily procure them; whereas for my sweet Chico they would give his weight in gold."

"His weight in gold!" reiterated Mrs. Raeburn, playing with her teaspoon; "think of that, Mark!"

"If that is the case, I should fatten him up well," observed the attorney, "and then sell him."

"Nay, but you would not, Mark," answered Brother Alec, quickly. "If I know your nature, it is to prefer affection and old associations to all the gold in the world. That poor bird has been my companion when I had no other, and has spoken my own tongue—you may laugh, but even his queer way of speaking it was better than nothing —when none could do the like within a thousand miles of me. There have been times when I have thought, 'When Chico dies, I shall lose my last friend.' I

would not part with him for a hundred
pounds."

"I wish you'd take something more, Mr.
Alexander, you are eating nothing!" exclaimed Mrs. Raeburn, persuasively. "Do
try that cutlet."

"I have quite done, thank you, dear
madam; but, if nobody is really going to
take it——"

"I am quite sure nobody is," answered
the hostess.

"So am I," remarked John, with confidence; "quite sure."

"Well, in that case, I'll give it to dear
old Fury here," said Brother Alec, and in
an instant the dainty morsel had disappeared
from human ken. There was no process of
mastication nor of deglutition; the dog's
enormous mouth opened and closed like that
of an automaton, and precisely the same
result would probably have taken place if
he had been offered a baby.

"Well, I call that sinful," ejaculated

Mrs. Raeburn, "to give good food to a dog. His way of taking it," added she more graciously, "shows, I fear, how dreadfully he has been spoilt, and also—does it not ?—by what a wealthy master he must have been brought up."

This was what in the law courts is called "a leading question," but, unfortunately, it failed of its effect.

"Well, I don't know as to that, dear madam," was the quiet reply. "I only saw his master for a few hours, and I never thought of asking him whether he had a balance at his banker's or not."

Mrs. Raeburn looked confused and disappointed. Forgetting that her brother-in-law had only purchased the dog two days ago she had hazarded a vital question, which, while it might reveal her own greedful curiosity, could not possibly elicit any satisfactory reply. The tone, too, of "Mr. Alexander," as she called him—and against the formality of which address he made no

protest, as he had done in Gertrude's case—
had been almost one of reproof.

If it was Mark Raeburn's intention, on
having obtained me for his articled clerk, to
get as much work out of me as possible, he
certainly showed no haste in exacting my
services. "You are free of the office, Sheddon, you know, and can take possession of
your high stool whenever you like," was the
not very pressing invitation that he gave
me, after breakfast, to commence my legal
studies; "or, perhaps, since it is a fine
morning," added he, "you would prefer a
stroll in the garden."

I thanked him, and chose the latter alternative; the more so, as I had from my
bed-room window seen Miss Floyd watering
the flowers, and noticed that the breakfast-
bell had called her away from an unfinished
task. I found her, as I had expected, still
among the lingering autumn roses, with a
bewitching little apron on to shield her
gown, and a pair of gardening gloves (pro-

bably Mrs. Raeburn's) much too large for
her fairy fingers, and which dropped from
them now and then, as though faint with
the ecstacy of inclosing such dainties. When
I ventured upon a high-flown compliment to
this effect, however, Miss Floyd only laughed
derisively, and presently observed, when one
of them fell into the water-pot, that, sup-
posing my view to be a correct one, it must
have committed suicide. Though Gertrude
had an appreciation of poetry, very rare in
Kirkdale folks, she had also a keen sense
of the ridiculous, which just then I felt
inclined to resent; for as a chance expression,
a glance, a gesture even, will sometimes in
one, however dear to us, remind us of
another with whom we are far from sympathetic, so her jesting seemed to me to
reflect the very man of whom I felt most
jealous—namely, John Raeburn; and the
idea at once suggested itself of hearing there
and then what the actual relations between
her and her young cousin really were. The

opportunity, however, was not easily found; or, perhaps, unwilling to exchange a state which, though of suspense, had still much eager hope in it, for one of blank disappointment, I was slow to press the matter. At all events, the water-pot was filled and emptied many times before I ventured to approach the subject. It came at last out of our talk about the new arrival, "Brother Alec," whom Gertrude pronounced to be a charming creature, simple and kind, and, for all his outlandish ways, a thorough gentleman.

"I am sure," said I, "the admiration is reciprocal; that is not surprising, of course, Miss Floyd?"

"Thank you, sir," interrupted she, with a delicious little courtesy. It was very provoking of her that she would not be serious.

"I say," continued I, "it is enough to make anybody jealous—that is, it would be so, if any one had a right to be jealous—

to see how affectionately the old gentleman regards you."

"Unhappily, I cannot attribute that to my own merits, Mr. Sheddon," answered she gravely. "It is the result of tender association. My mother, as I have heard, was at one time engaged to Mr. Alexander Raeburn."

"Indeed!" replied I; "then he must have been a very young lover, and your mother, I suppose, even younger."

"That was so," answered Gertrude, pensively.

"The custom seems to be hereditary in your family, Miss Floyd."

"What custom?"

The abruptness of the question startled me. I had flattered myself I had taken advantage of her confession to conduct my approaches very skilfully, and now it began to strike me that I had only been impertinent. However, it was too late to beat a retreat.

"I referred to the custom of early en-
gagements."

"Even now, Mr. Sheddon," answered she,
with a slight blush on her cheek, and con-
tinuing to douche a flower that had had
already much more than its share of water,
"I am at a loss to understand your
meaning."

Her manifest embarrassment confirmed
my suspicions, and gave me the courage of
despair.

"I have been given to understand, Miss
Floyd, though only yesterday" (and I laid
a pathetic stress upon those last two words),
"that you are yourself engaged to be
married."

She put down the water-pot, and confronted me with a steady look.

"Who told you that, Mr. Sheddon?"

I hesitated, doubting whether the question could have been justifiable which had
evidently given so keen an annoyance.

"I must insist upon a reply," continued

she, "or, if I may not insist, I implore you, as a gentleman, to answer me. Remember, sir, it is an orphaned girl who is appealing to you."

"Indeed, my dear Miss Floyd," protested I, "I had no idea of hurting your feelings. The information—which gave me great surprise, I own—came to me from a quarter that I could not doubt; your guardian, Mr. Mark Raeburn, told me so with his own lips."

"Mark Raeburn told you that I was engaged to be married! And pray, sir, to whom?"

"Well, unless I dreamt it, to his son John."

"That was false!" replied my companion, blushing to her very forehead. "False, and cowardly, and cruel."

She moved as though she would have returned within doors, and taxed at once the attorney with his baseness.

"One moment," said I, "dear Miss

Floyd "—the thought that any such rash
action might cause an immediate, and
perhaps eternal, separation between us flash-
ing upon me like the lightning that shows
the darkness of the night—"I may have
been mistaken as to his positively stating
the fact in question, though I have not a
shadow of doubt that he purposely led me
to conclude it. It was an infamous decep-
tion, and my own heart" (here I dropped
my voice, so that she might easily pretend
not to hear me, for it was far from my
wish now to precipitate matters) "reveals
the motive of it but too plainly. Still, it
would only bring confusion on my head to
reproach him with it. He would certainly
pretend that I must have misunderstood
him; while your own position in this house,
after such an explanation, would be rendered
to the last degree embarrassing."

The tears of mortification stood in my
fair companion's eyes, the blush of unde-
served shame dyed her modest cheeks; it

went to my heart to see her irresolution and distress; and the emergency made me wise beyond my years. "You are motherless, dear Miss Floyd," continued I, reading her bitter thoughts, "and without a friend under this roof, of your own sex, to advise or comfort you; but my Aunt Hastings, with all her faults, has a kindly heart, and would, I know, be a true friend to you if you would permit her. Should you be persecuted by the attentions of your cousin——"

"Forbear, sir, I entreat!" exclaimed Miss Floyd, earnestly. "You mean me well, I have no doubt, Mr. Sheddon, but it is not for you to offer me counsel. I do not yet know how I shall act with respect to what you have told me; but it is only fair to my cousin John to say, that neither directly nor indirectly has he lent himself, so far as I know, to the scheme—whether it be serious or pretended—at which you hint."

"Indeed," said I, with a sudden revulsion of feeling in favour of the family joker,

"I can easily believe it: John would never play so impudent a part. The utter absence of any outward pretension on his part to be the object of your choice would have made Mr. Raeburn's communication surprising to me, even if I myself had not ventured to hope that——"

"Hullo, hullo, hullo!" screamed a very high voice, proceeding from a very low level, and the ubiquitous Chico stood before us. He had waddled along the gravel walk that led from the house door, without attracting our attention. "This'll never do, you know; this'll never do," repeated he, shaking his scarlet head with portentous gravity, "Hullo, hullo, hullo!"

"I think you had better take Chico in, Mr. Sheddon, lest the cat should get at him," said Miss Floyd.

I at once understood from this—since Chico was obviously a match for any grimalkin at the Priory, and would have pecked out its eyes with gusto—that she wished our conversation to terminate for the present, which I was very willing it should do. If I had received no encouragement from her in that little fragment of a suit on which I had ventured, I had, at all events, met with no rebuff; while I had established a confidential relation between us which I felt to be eminently satisfactory. Above all, I had good cause to be content with the assurance I had had from her own lips, that no engagement existed between her and her cousin; nor did I, by any means, share her feelings of indignation against the attorney, whose unscrupulous assertion had had an effect exactly the reverse of what had been intended. So far from making me give up all hope of winning Gertrude, it had made me speak to her more plainly than, without it, I should have dared to do; while the object of his behaviour, which must needs now be as clear to her as it had been to me, might almost suffice, on my part, for a positive declaration of love.

I placed Chico, therefore, upon my wrist, as if he had been a love-bird, and having restored him to his master, betook myself to my desk in the office, not "to pen stanzas, when I should engross," but to hold a session of sweet thoughts, more engrossing far than the occupation which employed my fingers.

CHAPTER IX.

THE STORY OF UNCLE ALEC.

WHEN, after dinner that evening, we were all assembled in the drawing-room, Mrs. Raeburn, adopting the style of the sister to Scheherazadé in the Arabian Nights, thus addressed her guest and brother-in-law :

"Mr. Alexander, if you have nothing better to do to-night, I hope you will not refuse to relate what happened to you after quitting Richmond."

"By all means, my dear madam," returned he, good-naturedly, "and the more readily since it will give me the opportunity to relate the history of a little present or two, which I have brought with me for the accept-

ance of my dear friends here, and which
would have but little value save for the
story which attaches to them."

Mrs. Raeburn's countenance, which had
risen at the word "present," here fell again,
for "association" was not so attractive to
her practical mind as intrinsic worth : yet
she contrived to say, in her highly-principled
way, that nothing had been farther from her
mind than the personal advantage of herself
or of those belonging to her, in making her
request, and that it had been suggested to
her solely by the natural interest which she
felt in Mr. Alexander's wanderings.

"You are very good to say so, madam,"
returned the old man, with a bow, "and
I will not so ill repay you as to linger
over that part which, whatever its attractions
for myself, may easily seem tedious to those
who listen to me. My patron at Richmond
then, finding that I could reside no longer
under his roof with any pleasure to myself,
by reason of the public dislike with which

I was regarded, and at the same time filled with personal gratitude towards me for having rid him of so dangerous a neighbour as Redman, procured me employment elsewhere. A cousin of his had emigrated to Peru, where, in the neighbourhood of Cuzco, he had a large grazing farm, where herds of cattle were reared, chiefly for the supply of bulls for the Lima bull-ring, and this gentleman being in need of an English steward, Mr. Pittsburg recommended me for the situation. I gladly accepted his offer, and taking my credentials with me, which were couched in most friendly and flattering terms, I travelled by way of Panama to Lima, and thence on mule-back, the only means of transit across the Cordillera of the Andes. In that district inns are (or were at that period) utterly unknown, but the most unbounded hospitality is on every hand to be met with. If each householder had been my brother, like yourself, Mark, I could not have been received with greater kindness. The magnificence of

the mountain scenery, the glorious climate,
the richness of the pasture lands, the fertility
of the ravines and valleys, and, above all—
though my then ignorance of Spanish placed
me at a great disadvantage in this respect
—the legends of past greatness and splen-
dour that environ almost every locality in
the country of the Incas, gave to every
day of my journey the aspect of a gorgeous
dream. In the recesses of that Sierra, as
doubtless you all have heard, lay concealed the
inexhaustible and far-famed treasures of Peru."

"And has nobody found them yet?"
inquired Mrs. Raeburn, pertinently.

"Some have been found, madam, but
most of them will doubtless remain undis-
covered for all time. The fact of their existence was in each case intrusted to as few
persons as possible, and those persons being
poor Indians, whose lives—entirely at the
mercy of their Spanish masters—have too
often been sacrificed, when their secret
perished with them."

"What on earth did they go burying their money for, instead of putting it in the bank?" inquired the attorney, whose historical knowledge was by no means on a par with his commercial experience.

"Well, Mark, there were two reasons. In the first place, the Indian belief in a place of future rewards and punishments, combined with their loyalty, led to the burial of vast treasures along with their dead princes."

"I see," said Mark, "they thought it, as Rogers the banker observed when he heard that a friend had died worth half a million, 'a pretty sum to begin the next world with.'"

"Just so. Moreover, the vast wealth of the temples had been in many cases hidden in a similar manner, in order to escape the cupidity of the Spaniards. Even the mouths of silver mines were stopped up, and all traces of their existence done away with, so that the hated conquerors should reap no advantage from them; nor could the pain of torture nor the fear of death wring the secret from those who held it. The Spanish yoke had not been thrown off at the time of my arrival, and every tongue that dared to wear it was tipped with the fire of indignation against them. I could tell you tales, dear madam," said Brother Alec, addressing Mrs. Raeburn, gravely, "of such fiendish cruelty and oppression inflicted by these foreign conquerors, as would cause you not only to abhor them as the fiend himself, but to regard the system under which alone such deeds were possible—that of slavery—as hateful in the sight of God and man."

It was evident enough that "Uncle Alec" was greatly moved, so Mrs. Raeburn, instead of debating the matter, which she doubtless felt much impelled to do, framed what she conceived to be a conciliatory reply, as follows:

"Well, well, Mr. Alexander, I have no

doubt there is something to be said on both sides of the question."

"I can tell you what is to be said on one side, madam," continued Uncle Alec, sternly; "that between the time of the Incas and the year of Liberty in 1828—that is, in three hundred years—the native population of Peru was reduced by five millions of souls, in consequence of their compulsory mine service and its hideous conditions of starvation, stripes, and darkness. Nay, I can tell you one crime of my own knowledge, which was committed upon a man, himself a Spaniard, and from the lips of whose son I myself heard it. There was a certain poor man, named Don Pedro Giron, who was a physician, and who, quite contrary to the usual habit of his countrymen, had endeared himself to the Indians by acts of benevolence and the gratuitous practice of his art; and having by his skill saved a young Indian boy from death, the grateful father disclosed to his benefactor the existence

of a certain mine in Pinco. The Spanish
viceroy envying him his newly-acquired
wealth, cast him into prison, upon some
groundless charge of fomenting rebellion
among the natives, and refused to forward
his appeal to the Spanish king, even though
he offered to give him a bar of pure silver
daily while the ship went from Callao to
Europe and back, a voyage that lasted at
that time six months. The tyrant, however, over-reached himself by his own cruelty,
since Don Pedro died under the sufferings
inflicted on him, and never disclosed the
whereabouts of the source of his wealth."

"And what became of it eventually—
I mean the mine?" inquired Mrs. Raeburn.
"Was it ever discovered?"

"It was never publicly made known,
madam," answered Brother Alec, drily,
"though I have seen it with these eyes."

A total silence followed upon this statement; even volatile John Raeburn appeared
fascinated by the attraction of his uncle's

words and manner, which were singularly pregnant and suggestive ; while the rapt attention which his hostess bestowed upon them would have been a compliment to the best *raconteur* in Europe.

"There is more than one curious story connected with that Pinco mine," continued Brother Alec, as though in acknowledgment of our interest in the topic, "which are less widely known than that connected with poor Pedro Giron. A certain Franciscan monk, who was a gambler, had done some good service to a native, who, in return, presented him with a large bag of silver ore. His cupidity was at once excited, and taxing the Indian with the knowledge of a concealed mine, he besought him to let him behold it, promising the most solemn secrecy, and that he would never revisit it upon his own account. The Indian assented, and accompanied by two others, blindfolded the monk, and carried him up by night into the mountains, where

he eventually showed him a subterranean
gallery sparkling with silver ore. On his
return the cunning monk loosened his beads
one by one, and dropped them on the road,
with the intention of retracing it by means
of them; but in the morning the Indian
returned with a whole handful of them, and
the significant remark, 'Good father, you
have dropped your breviary;' so that he
had to keep his word in spite of himself."

"And may I ask, dear Mr. Alexander,"
observed our hostess, in her most conciliatory
manner, "how it was that you yourself
contrived to gain admission to this wondrous mine?"

Brother Alec here grew very grave.

"Indeed, madam, I fear I must keep
that secret, as poor Don Pedro kept his,
inviolable. The circumstances, too, were,
after all, of a private nature, and had no
such striking features about them as belónged
to the cases I have mentioned."

"There was a woman at the bottom of

it, I'll lay ten pounds," cried the attorney, boisterously. The presence of his brother at the dinner-table had enabled him to make more free with the sherry than was usually possible ; though, on the other hand—perhaps out of the fear of losing that relative's good opinion—the brandy bottle had not made its appearance at dessert. "Come, Alec, I can see by your face that I have hit the blot."

In Peru backgammon was probably unknown, and the metaphor thus drawn from that amusement may therefore have been unintelligible to one from whose memory the fireside games of his own country must long ago have faded out. Over Alec's brow passed the first cloud that I had seen shadow it, as he replied, "There was no blot in the case, Mark, I am thankful to say ; though you are right in so far that a woman was concerned in it—the brightest and loveliest creature that ever blessed earth with her presence, and who, having departed from it, has robbed life, for me, of all its charms."

His voice had such an exquisite pathos in it, infinitely more touching from its welling through those white-bearded lips, that I heard John Raeburn mutter pitifully, "Poor old buffer," and saw the tears rise in Gertrude's eyes. Alec, whose glance had turned towards her while he spoke the last sentence, as though to a quarter where he could count on sympathy, saw them also. "I had loved before, it is true," continued he, addressing her in a gentle apologetic tone, "but Fate had long separated me from the object of my boyish passion. I felt no sting of conscience, cousin Gertrude, when I married my Indian bride."

"Indian bride!" ejaculated Mrs. Raeburn, like an echo, shocked. "Were such matches usual in Peru, Mr. Alexander?"

"Unhappily, madam, they were not. This girl, who had the blood of Huayna Ccapac, the greatest of the Incas, in her veins, would not by some have been deemed worthy to be allied to a penniless adventurer like myself, who chanced to be of European descent."

"Then this young woman was not penniless," remarked Mrs. Raeburn simply; "that, of course, made the match much less unequal."

"Yes, madam ; it made it a still greater condescension on her side. I was but a rich man's steward, well-to-do indeed by that time, but whose means, beside those which Inez Nusta could command, were contemptible indeed. When I married her, however, I am thankful to say, I knew not of their existence. I had heard that she was descended from the noblest family in Peru, and one which had at one time been its rulers, but I little suspected that she was their heiress. Her father saw me woo and win her, like a man of honour, though I was of the white-skinned race, and when I married her, he, out of gratitude, disclosed

to me that he owned the silver mine in
Pinco, and had inherited those buried treasures of the Huatanay, the knowledge of
whose hiding-place had entailed death and
torture on so many of his race."

"Would it be a breach of confidence,
Alec, to tell us what was the Huatanay?"
inquired the attorney, his native humour,
which still occasionally manifested itself in
spite of his wife's depressing sway, being
doubtless stimulated by these disclosures of
his brother's prosperity.

"The Huatanay is a river, beneath whose
channel, it had always been whispered, lay
somewhere hidden the golden fittings of the
Temple of the Sun at Cuzco, which the
Spaniards had found stripped of its splendours. They had plundered the shrine of
Pachacamac, in the neighbourhood of Lima,
of its enormous riches, the contributions of
ten generations of worshippers; they had
stripped its doors of their golden plates,
and its ceilings of their precious stones, and

out of its silver ornaments had even paved
a road for miles for the triumphant passage
of their viceroy; but with the temple at
Cuzco the natives had been beforehand with
them. Its central door and massive cornice
were said to have been of virgin gold; the
Sacred Sun, in whose honour the edifice
had been reared, was made of the same
metal, studded with emeralds and turquoises,
and shone like its namesake in the firma-
ment; its vases of gold, supposed to repre-
sent the tears shed by that luminary, stood
filled with sacrificial first-fruits on its costly
floor; but none of these ever gladdened the
greedy eyes of Pizarro or De Castro."

To behold Mrs. Raeburn at that moment
was a commentary on the speaker's words
such as is rarely indeed supplied to text.
I had somewhere read of a miser, whose
pulse would rise to fever quickness at the
mention of any large sum of money; and
it really seemed, to judge by the eager and
hungry looks of our hostess, that he had

found his parallel in her. At the mention of the silver mines her countenance had exhibited a force of expression of which I should have deemed it utterly incapable, but while she listened to the catalogue of these golden splendours, it had become positively eloquent with rapacity and greed. Uncle Alec, however, saw nothing of this; his thoughts were rapt in the topics on which he was discoursing, and his eyes, fixed straight before him, were evidently regarding a far other scene than that around him. He looked up, like one aroused from a dream, when Mrs. Raeburn inquired, with earnest vehemence :

"And do you mean to say, dear Mr. Alexander, that you yourself beheld these wondrous treasures, and handled all those precious things with your own fingers ?"

"I handled some, madam, and saw them all," replied he, quietly. "If proofs be needed of what indeed may easily seem to be a gorgeous romance, I possess them here." He took from his pocket a leather bag, and out of it some articles carefully wrapped up in leather. "Here are three images of various sizes," said he, "yet very literally (as I was saying yesterday of Chico) worth their weight in gold, since they *are* gold. Their workmanship is not such as we are accustomed to admire in Europe; yet I doubt not, independent of their intrinsic worth, these weird fantastic figures, so many ages old, would have a value in the eyes of antiquarians equal to the best products of Grecian or Italian art."

"Are you sure it is really gold?" asked Mrs. Raeburn, with a voice that fairly trembled with emotion, as she took the largest of the images into her hand.

"I am quite sure, madam," answered Brother Alec, smiling. "If it were counterfeit, I should not venture, as I do, to beg your acceptance of it."

"Why, this must be worth a matter of a hundred pounds," ejaculated Mrs. Raeburn, forgetting, in her intense appreciation of its value, to acknowledge the gift itself.

"I don't know as to that, madam," returned he. "I only know that you are very welcome to it. Brother Mark, here is one for you, which I am sure you will value for my sake, even if you have no love for antiquities. Cousin Gertrude, this is but a little one, but its size does not typify the affection with which I regard you for your dear mother's sake. I only wish I had brought more, that no one here should have been empty-handed," and the old man looked at John and me with quite a distressed air.

"I am sure you have been more than generous enough already," observed our hostess, regarding her costly present much as some devotee might have done, in whose eyes it had been a genuine divinity. "It is not to be expected that you should have burthened your personal luggage with many such articles. You turned most of the pro-

perty of this kind into a more portable
form, doubtless, before you left the land of
the Incas."

"Indeed, I did not, madam ; long before
I quitted Cuzco there was happily no occasion for any man to conceal the wealth
which he had honestly come by. The bulk
of what I possessed was in bars of silver,
for which, as I was told, I could get a larger
sum at the Mint in London than from the
bankers in Lima."

"And what an enormous weight it must
have been, Mr. Alexander."

"It was certainly very heavy, madam ;
indeed, my chief difficulty lay in getting a
strong box to carry it, and sufficiently power-
ful tackle to convey it on board ; the ship
was in deep water, and if a handle had
broken away, or a chain snapped, I must
have wished 'good-bye' to what, even in
Peru, was considered a considerable fortune."

"But the handles stood fast, and the
chains held, I trust, Mr. Alexander ?"

"They did so, madam; and the box lies at my agents' in London."

Not another question did Mrs. Raeburn put to her brother-in-law, after this interesting point had been so satisfactorily settled; but Gertrude, who sat beside him, had much to ask concerning his Peruvian life, to which he very willingly replied. His description of the country, with its splendid scenery, its thickets of mollé trees, its noble fuchsias covered with crimson flowers, its roadways carpeted with heliotropes and blue and scarlet salvias, had a peculiar charm for her, to whom the pleasures of the garden were an unfailing delight; nor did her interest fail when he spoke of his duties at the cattle farm, and of his gradual acquisition of an independence.

Presently he dropped his voice, so that Gertrude alone could hear him, but in the gentle and sympathising expression of her face, it was easy for me at least to read that he was discoursing of his Indian bride, whom he had wooed in his far-back youth, and won to find her a richer prize than all her unlooked-for wealth, only to lose her at last for ever.

CHAPTER X.

I HAVE said that Mrs. Raeburn no longer
thought it necessary to put her brother-in-
law through any cross-examination as to his
affairs; but from the hour of the discovery
of his being a wealthy man, she plied him
with endless questions concerning his personal comforts. He had only to express a
wish respecting the arrangement of his room,
the time at which he preferred to take his
meals, and his preference to a particular dish
at any one of them, to have it gratified. She
well reconsidered within herself that question
of his smoking in bed, and on her reflecting
that the house and furniture were insured to

their full value, and that if any accident did occur, he would surely see the propriety of handsomely recompensing the family for the inconvenience, she withdrew her objection to that custom. On the very next morning after that narration of his adventures, the fatted calf—in the mitigated form of a couple of kidneys—was served up for the breakfast of this honoured guest, and great was the chagrin of his hostess when he only took a fourth of that costly dish, as being, when the two ladies had declined to partake of it, neither more nor less than his proper share. In vain did she wink hard at her husband and her son; they were neither of them inclined to deny themselves so unusual a dainty; while, as for myself, I considered it as included in my one hundred and fifty pounds per annum, and would probably have done so (as Mrs. Raeburn afterwards observed to John in confidence, who, as a matter of course, retailed it to me) "had it been nightingales' tongues."

In consequence of this generous forbearance on the part of Brother Alec, the general
supply of these extras was largely increased,
so that we all benefited from his sister-in-
law's desire to please him, and blessed the
hour in which he threw himself on her
prodigal hospitality. There was really no
limit to her endeavours to gratify his tastes,
his palate, and even those inconvenient fancies,
from which no man, who has sojourned long
in foreign climes, is wholly free. The serpents
had their bread and milk, and performed
their evolutions as they pleased, the only
stipulation being that they should remain in
Mr. Alexander's apartment, except when he
occasionally played Laocoon with them in
the drawing-room, for the public amusement;
the bull-dog eat his weight in beefsteaks
twice a day; and the parrot was allowed to
indulge in a vocabulary that was more ex-
tensive than select, at any hour of the day
or night, not even excepting Sundays. Every
doubt of her brother-in-law's being a wealthy

man had been swept away from her mind, if not from the moment when he had presented her with that precious example of Peruvian handiwork, at all events from that in which the Kirkdale jeweller, whom she consulted on the subject without delay, assured her that it was genuine gold. The reflection that she had judged rightly in this matter, while her husband had doubted, was also a source of intense satisfaction to her; and although Mrs. Raeburn was scarcely one of those persons who are said to be "very agreeable when pleased," her manners were modified by the circumstance, and at least presented a pleasing contrast to what they had been before her guest's arrival.

Another source of congratulation with her was the importance that the family acquired in the neighbourhood from their possession of Brother Alec, the report of whose untold wealth spread far and wide, enriching the social soil as such news is wont to do, so that acquaintanceships sprang

up where none had hitherto existed, and in
some cases even yielded welcome fruit in
the form of "an increased legal connection."
Mr. and Mrs. Raeburn had more invitations
to dinner during the next five months—
thanks to the companion they took with
them—than they had received during the
same number of years. This new-born
popularity, however, had its drawbacks in
the necessity it entailed of a reciprocity of
hospitality; and many a feast had the re-
luctant mistress of the Priory to provide in
which her ginger-wine could not play its
thrifty part, and the feathered grasses that
had been wont to furnish forth her frugal
table were compelled to give way to the
foamy wine for which Brother Alec had expressed his decided preference. His natural
and matter-of-course acceptance of all the
favours which she lavished upon him would
have been intolerable to her, did she not
count it as so much corroboration of his
possession of those ample means with which

he was on all hands credited; but with other persons his simple, unaffected manners were highly popular. My Uncle Ralph, in particular, who was among the first to congratulate him upon his return to England, delighted in his company; while my aunt was reported to have expressed a suspicion that Brother Alec was an impostor, who, from some misplaced ambition, had essayed to play the part of a Raeburn, but who was, in reality, much too "nice" to be related to the family. He was certainly very nice. Tender, gentle, and generous, with such a genial air as charmed his hearers, and a graphic power of describing what he had seen that evinced no common intellectual powers; but he was also very eccentric. He had a habit of twitching so violently when suffering under verbal chastisement—long bucolic stories from the country gentlemen, or protracted discourses from the Kirkdale pulpit—that you might have judged him to be afflicted by St. Vitus's dance;

while, when moved to indignation by some after-dinner antagonist—this was especially the case when any tyrannical or oppressive system was being apologised for or defended —he was accustomed, before his turn came to reply, to emit guttural noises expressive of dissatisfaction and disgust, of the utterance of which he was wholly unconscious.

It is needless to say that these salient points, as also many other peculiarities of tone and manner, were seized upon by John Raeburn, and imitated to perfection. The family likeness, of which his mother had spoken, between the uncle and nephew was quite strong enough, to begin with, to utterly demolish my Aunt Hastings's theory. Then John was thin and spare, and had an old face ; so that, but for the white hair and beard, you might easily have imagined, when this undutiful lad was giving his imitations, that his Uncle Alec was addressing you in person. The best of it was, that nobody appreciated this performance better than the

individual who was thus travestied ; and
many a hearty laugh did he enjoy at his
own expense while John twitched and grunted
at an imaginary antagonist, or lavished on
Chico the absurdly-endearing epithets that
were wont to be applied to him by his
devoted master.   The dismal Priory was,
in fact, transformed by Uncle Alec's genial
presence, and by the fun that grew out
of it, into quite an agreeable place of residence ; and as the attorney by no means
overtasked me with legal duties, and the
relations between myself and Gertrude, though
tacit, grew every day more tender and confidential, I, for my part, had no cause to
complain of my lot.   If it were my purpose, indeed, to be my own biographer, I
should here, though but for a brief space, be
narrating how the course of true love did
run smooth, and everything bade fair to
make two lovers happy ; but this story has
not myself, but others, for its theme, though
I and she, who was dearer than myself ;

chanced to have the thread of our lives mingled with theirs.

There was one thing only that disturbed Mrs. Racburn's complacent satisfaction with the position of affairs—namely, that up to this date not a word had passed her brother-in-law's lips respecting the agreement made between him and Mark in their far-back youth, which, for all her husband's confidence in Brother Alec's sense of its moral obligation, she was very desirous to hear him acknowledge. Had he been the one likely to be advantaged by a division of profits, he would have been eager enough, she reasoned, to advert to the subject; and so far his silence was not displeasing to her; but there were other matters which made her impatient for what my Uncle Hastings called Alec's Declaration of Independence. The rector, it will be remembered, had been admitted to the secret on the same occasion with myself, when the attorney, warmed with wine, and confident that he would never set eyes on his long-lost relative again, had beguiled our after-dinner time with its narration; but a sense of delicacy had not only restrained him from communicating it to others, but had caused him to enjoin on me a similar reticence. No one, therefore, beyond the family circle at the Priory, was aware of the peculiar position in which the two brothers stood; folks looked upon the wanderer's return as a piece of probable good fortune for the Raeburns in the future indeed (provided the new-comer continued to find his relatives to his satisfaction), but of no immediate pecuniary advantage to them, save what might arise from the general belief in their great expectations. This, as I have said, was already considerable; but it was counterbalanced by a singular circumstance. Brother Alec was for ever applying to the attorney for small sums of money, which, as it happened, it was not very convenient for him to lend; the fact that the former had not paid a

single bill, except his washing bill, since his
arrival, and that the tailor and the bootmaker
in Kirkdale had sent in their little accounts
without effect for rigging him out in the
European style, excited no suspicion of his
schemes in Mrs. Raeburn's mind; her own
feelings upon money matters made her well
understand that the richer a man is the
more unwilling he often is to part with
coin, even to pay his just debts; but the
borrowing of those small sums from her
husband—or, rather, from herself, since she
held the purse-strings—did trouble her very
much. Brother Alec's enormous wealth could
not surely consist so exclusively in bars of
silver and golden images that he did not
know where to find a five-pound note, or
even a sovereign; and the parting with these
little sums was, to her, like bleeding slowly
to death in a warm bath; she perspired and
grew faint with the hideous apprehension,
fanciful though she knew it was, that she
might possibly never get them back again.

She was well aware of the risk that lay in pressing the great question, "And now, Mr. Alexander, rich as you are, are you prepared to carry out the solemn covenant made with my husband more than a generation ago, to halve the goods with which Fortune has dowered you?" It was likely enough he would at once suspect her interested designs, and put down all the favours he had received from her to their true account; but, still, her patience was almost worn out, and his trespasses upon her purse—and not the less because they were generally made to purchase some present, or provide some treat, for the young folks in the neighbourhood, of whom Brother Alec was the idol, so that all went out of the family—were getting well-nigh intolerable.

An application of her brother-in-law for a five-pound note, to be spent in fireworks on Gertrude's birthday, at Easter time, was the last drop that caused Mrs. Raeburn's cup of bitterness to overflow, which it did in the drawing-room amongst us all, with an effect that I shall never forget to my dying day, and with such consequential results as, could I have foreseen them, would have impressed me even more.

"Five pounds for fireworks!" remonstrated she; "that is throwing money into the fire indeed, Mr. Alexander. Of course, I cannot tell how rich you are; you are so very reticent about your own affairs; but, unless you are a millionaire, I must confess that to spend such a sum in squibs and crackers seems abominable!"

"A millionaire!" exclaimed Brother Alec. "You must be laughing at me, my dear madam."

"Well, I mean you ought to have hundreds of thousands of pounds to make so light of five-pound notes as you do."

"Hundreds of thousands of pounds!" repeated Brother Alec, vacantly; while Chico on his shoulder, catching his tone as usual, cried, "Oh dear! oh dear! oh dear! oh dear! Only think of that."

"My dear madam, I have scarce a hundred thousand pence!"

"Why, that's only four hundred and sixteen pounds, thirteen shillings and fourpence!" shrieked Mrs. Raeburn, who was "a ready reckoner" and a "save-all" in one. "You are joking, Mr. Alexander, I know," added she, with a ghastly smile; "but I am not fond of joking upon these important matters."

"I never was more serious in my life, madam," answered Brother Alec, and indeed he looked not only serious but exceedingly distressed. "You talk of my reticence concerning my own affairs, but Mark can explain how that was, if he will. It was for him to speak, not for me. I confess I understood from your manner, madam, that you yourself—nay, I may add that all present here, were aware of the agreement that existed between him and me, of which I am certain"—here he looked tenderly towards his brother—"Mark will never question the validity; but if that is not so, I must at once tell you that your husband and I made a solemn compact when we parted in our youth, that when we met again each should give the other the one half of whatever property he might then be possessed of, so that God should bless us both alike. Was it for me, an unsuccessful adventurer, to remind Mark of it, or to wait his own good time to advert to it?"

"An unsuccessful adventurer!" gasped Mrs. Raeburn, while her husband's face turned from red to white, and his eyes seemed about to start from their sockets. "Why, how much was in that iron box that you told us was at your agents' in London?"

"When it left shore, madam, about twelve thousand pounds' worth of silver metal, which, unfortunately, lies sixty fathoms deep in Lima harbour. The handles and chains held well enough, as I told you, but, unhappily, the bottom of the box came out as it was being swung on board."

"Then you purposely led us to believe that you were a wealthy man, when, in fact, you had lost your all, sir," said Mrs. Raeburn with slow distinctness, and a certain terrible expression in her pale. face which I can only describe as the white heat of hatred.

"If it be an offence, madam, not to anticipate a question, I own I am so far guilty," returned the other, with dignity. "To all your very pertinent inquiries I gave you a truthful answer; but I confess they jarred upon my feelings, since their mercenary object was only too obvious to me. It wounded me to the core to find my brother's wife concerned herself in no wise in my affairs, but only as to the amount of property that I might have brought home for her behoof. Had Mark asked me for my confidence, it would have been given to him unreservedly, and at once. I should have said, as I still say to him, notwithstanding your cruel words, 'I have returned a poor man, but I will never make you poor, Mark. You are a family man, and I will not exact from you the conditions of our agreement. Keep your wealth, undivided; only give me a home in your own house, and a comfortable subsistence there— I happen to know, brother, that I shall not be long a tax upon its hospitality— until I die.'"

These words were addressed so directly to the attorney that he could no longer delegate the task of reply to his Matilda. He looked up hurriedly from the floor, on which his gaze had been fixed, and with an abashed, uneasy air, observed, "I really think you are greatly to blame, Alec, in this matter. You had no right to deceive us as to the state of your affairs. Your welcome would have been just as hearty had you made a clean breast of it; though

you would not, perhaps, have been entertained in so lavish a manner. There is
little, indeed, on the score of loss with
which to reproach you." (Here he looked
at his wife and held his hand up, seeing
that she was about to burst into a furious
denial.) "The golden images which you
gave to Matilda and myself will doubtless
repay any cost to which we may have been
put upon your account; but of course things
must now be placed on quite another footing.
The entertainment of your animal friends
is, to begin with, a serious item in our
domestic expenditure."

"Do you hear that, my darling?" murmured Brother Alec, pathetically, to his
feathered favourite; "they grudge you your
nuts and oranges."

"Oh dear! oh dear! oh dear!" answered
the parrot.

"Chico is right, Alec," said the attorney,
whose voice was growing more confident with
every word, since he found himself uninter-

rupted by his wife, and perceived his brother
submissive; "such things are very dear, when
given to birds. Of course your home is here,
so long as you choose to live with us, but
these extra expenses must be cut off: it has
long distressed Mrs. Raeburn to see so much
good food thrown away on dogs and reptiles.
I am afraid she will insist—and I cannot
blame her for it—upon a change being
made, at once, in this respect. Is it not
so, Matilda?"

"So absurd a question requires no answer,
Mr. Raeburn," was that lady's grim reply;
"but when you have quite done, I have a
few words to say."

"Do not speak them; I pray you do not
speak them, madam," cried Brother Alec, in
a low beseeching voice. "No words that
you can utter can do more than what has
been already done. I have been told by
poor tortured creatures in Peru, that when
their bodies have been beaten with great
severity, blows hurt them no more, since the

bruised flesh becomes deadened to the pain; and so it is now, madam, with my heart. I acknowledge that I was wrong to intrude my presence here——"

"Upon false pretences," put in the attorney, mildly.

"Upon the misunderstanding rather that I was a wealthy man, Mark," continued the other; "whereas I had no claim on your hospitality, save that I was your brother, returned, as it must have seemed to you, out of the mouth of the grave."

"That claim I allow," answered the attorney, with unaccustomed firmness, and striking his hand upon the table. "I will not have you turned out of house and home, though you should not possess a penny piece."

Mrs. Raeburn gave a contemptuous snort.

"Yes, I swear it," continued Mark; "but, at the same time, we cannot afford to minister to your luxurious habits. More-over, it was highly reprehensible in you to borrow money of Mrs. Raeburn, which, it seems, you are hardly in a position to repay. You owe bills, too, Alec, as I understand, in the town?"

"A few pounds, Mark, yes; and as much again, perhaps, I have borrowed of your wife," returned the other, quietly. "Still, what were they when, by our solemn compact—which, I protest to Heaven, I believe you have acknowledged all along, and would have gladly put into effect if I had been the rich man you supposed me to be—the one-half of all you had was mine. Do you ignore that compact? Do you deny that obligation?"

"The man is mad!" exclaimed Mrs. Raeburn, scornfully.

"Mark, it is to *you* I speak," cried Brother Alec, stretching out his hand with earnest dignity. "In the presence of your own flesh and blood, here, who will take his lesson of justice from your lips—and before these young folks, who know, because truth

is in them, what your answer ought to be
—I ask you, once for all, do you admit
the fact of the agreement to which I have
referred, and do you hold it binding on you ?"

"My dear Alec," returned the attorney,
fixing his eyes on a corner of the drawing-
room table-cloth and taking its tassel in his
hand, "I do not deny that, when we were
boys——"

"Not boys, Mark."

"Well, very young men then ; of age, it
is true, but not of that mature age which
alone is adapted—and—and—suitable for
arrangements involving the interests of a
lifetime, we did make the romantic compact
to which you refer ; but as to its being
binding, my dear Alec, in the sense that
we lawyers are accustomed to attach to that
word, you must forgive me if I say that
your long absence from England, and your
residence in a semi-barbarous country, can
alone account for your entertaining such a
preposterous idea."

"I see," said Brother Alec, in a low and broken voice; "I see. Do not pain yourself and me by saying more. No, madam" —for Mrs. Raeburn here began with her "Mr. Alexander"—"I cannot hear you either. I have heard enough. If it is not too expensive a luxury, I wish to go to bed."

This brief return of the old greybeard's humour was even more sad than his pathos had been: his mouth, which tried to force a smile, twitched and quivered so, that I half feared it was the prelude to a stroke of paralysis. He got up feebly from his chair, and moved slowly across the room, like one who travels in the dark.

Gertrude followed him swiftly, and gave him her arm so far as the drawing-room door.

"Thanks, Gerty," said he; "thanks, my darling, your poor relation will not trouble you for long. Will he, Chico?"

"Dead! dead! dead!" answered the parrot.

CHAPTER XI.

WE five in the drawing-room stared at one another in silence, while the voice of the bird, repeating its monotonous cry of "Dead! dead! dead!" grew fainter and fainter, each filled with our own reflections upon the scene that had just occurred. I, for my part, was blaming myself for not having run forward, as Gertrude had done, to assist the old man, and also for not having expressed a syllable of the sympathy I felt for him in every throb of my pulses; though, after all, he might have taken any verbal interference on my part as an impertinence, since I was but a lad in years, no relation of the family,

and not even in the independent position
of a guest, since I was but his brother's
articled clerk. Moreover, if I had spoken,
I should certainly have expressed an indignation which would have done poor Brother
Alec no good service. Nevertheless, as I
have said, I felt distressed and ashamed,
and when presently Mrs. Racburn broke the
silence by thus addressing me: "And now,
I suppose, Mr. Sheddon, you will be telling
this discreditable story all over the town,"
I endeavoured to make up for my past
cowardice.

"I am no tale-bearer, Mrs. Raeburn,"
answered I, "and shall always honourably
keep secret such private matters as come
to my knowledge in this house; but I must
be permitted to say that the word 'discreditable' does not seem to me to apply
to Mr. Alexander Raeburn's conduct in this
affair, however well it may describe that of
others."

"You are very welcome to your opinion,

young man," answered Mrs. Raeburn, contemptuously, "though your expression of it
does not show much respect for your master
yonder."

"Tush, tush!" exclaimed the attorney,
pettishly, "the boy is quite right to stand
up for his friend. There is, after all, something to be said upon poor Alec's side."

"Indeed, sir! Well, at all events, there
is no necessity to argue the matter in public,"
observed Mrs. Raeburn, with a glance of
wrath at her husband that said, "Silence,
fool!" as plainly as any words.

"Yes, but this is not in public, Matilda,"
returned the attorney, who had his own
reasons for making terms for his brother
while he had a sympathising audience at his
back, rather than in the sacred but unsafe
solitude of the connubial chamber. "Mr.
Sheddon here, who is a young gentleman of
honour, has pledged himself to secrecy upon
this matter, and for the rest we are all of
one family. Gertrude is Alec's relative as

well as my own, and it is but right that
she should hear the end of this affair as
well as the beginning. You and my brother
never hit it off together from the first, and
prejudice should not be allowed to interfere
with judgment."

" Judgment!" echoed Mrs. Raeburn, with
a shrill laugh, like the noise made by
the escape-pipe from a railway engine, and
without which means of relief she perhaps,
like it, would have been in danger of bursting. "Here is an impostor, who, by a false
representation of his position, has caused us
to turn our house out of doors to please him,
to harbour wild beasts and reptiles, to lavish
champagne like water, to lend him five-
pound notes to make paper kites of—for he
has spent most of it in toys ; and I, forsooth,
am to use judgment ! It would be much
more to the purpose to send for a police-
man, and I've half a mind to do it."

A stifled cry of horror broke from Gertrude's lips.

"Well, it's only for your sake, my dear cousin, if I don't," added Mrs. Raeburn, clutching at this gracious method of extricating herself from what she must have felt to be a ridiculous position.

As for John, he was breathing very hard, with his handkerchief stuffed into his mouth, and his eyes protruding like a lobster's. The notion of Uncle Alec in the custody of Sergeant Tims, of the county police—a figure familiar to him at Quarter Sessions—on the charge of obtaining champagne under false pretences, was evidently tickling his heart-strings.

"You are talking rubbish, Matilda!" exclaimed the attorney, angrily, "and what, if it were not rubbish, would be exceedingly disgraceful." His irritation was perhaps as much feigned as real, for it was only by getting into a passion, or pretending to be in one, that he could ever muster courage to oppose himself to his formidable spouse. "I say now, once for all, notwithstanding all that has come and gone, that I will not have my own brother turned out of my own house; so, if that is what you've got in your mind, Matilda, dismiss it."

"I was not thinking of turning your brother out of your own house, as you call it, Mark; though, in that matter, it is much less yours than mine."

"Be silent, woman!" exclaimed the attorney, menacingly, and rising hastily from his chair. "I spoke of what was in your mind, but it strikes me you are clean gone out of it."

There was a dreadful silence at these words, the vehemence and rage of which (by no means simulated this time) seemed to have its effect even on Mrs. Raeburn.

"I am quite sane, thank you, Mark," returned she, coldly.

"Then perhaps you will be good enough to state your plans," observed her husband. "Let us hear them once for all; I won't be worried and bullyragged about this matter

all night, I promise you. I have done quite
enough this evening out of deference to your
opinion. There is going to be some com-
promise on your part too, I hope?"

"Our course seems to me quite obvious,
Mr. Raeburn. As to turning Mr. Alexander
out of doors, that is an idea which never
occurred to me. He must, of course, stay
on here for the present; he has a claim upon
you to that extent, I allow; but I suppose
I shall be justified in treating him as one
of the family—not as a prince of the blood
royal? It is only reasonable to expect re-
payment of the sums I have advanced him
on the faith of his representation; and of
course I shall insist on the disposal of his
horrible animals. For the rest, we must
take our time to consider of it and talk the
matter over.—John, please to light my bed
candle."

The attorney turned pale and shivered.
"John," said he, "bring me the brandy."

It was the first time that he had ever

ventured to call for that liquor in his wife's
presence. He did so now, I think, to give
her notice that on that night at least a cur-
tain-lecture would be thrown away upon him.
He felt like a beaten general who has to
fall back upon his reserves.

"My dear Gertrude," observed Mrs. Raeburn, significantly, "I think you had better
retire also, since a brandy bottle is about to
be brought into the drawing-room."

The two ladies withdrew together, and
then the attorney rang for hot water and
tumblers, and having brewed some punch,
poured out a glass for each of us.

"This is a sad business, Sheddon," said
he. "I own to you that, if I had not the
utmost confidence in your honour, I should
feel greatly disturbed about it. If the
rumour got abroad that poor Alec was a
pauper, it would be very grievous to me—
I mean, of course," he added hastily, "in
the way of social humiliation. Poor Mrs.
Raeburn has gone about, as women will do,

boasting of her rich brother-in-law, and she naturally feels bitter about it. It is, I own, a disappointment to myself—a great disappointment." Here he drained his glass, and poured himself out another. "I don't think my brother meant to deceive us, Sheddon; upon my life I don't. Money matters had never any attraction for him, and he imagines that that is the case with others. He thought that it could not much signify to us whether he was a rich man or a poor one; nor would it have done so in the sense of our affection for, or behaviour towards him. Heaven forbid! but it caused us to entertain expectations. There has been no positive loss, as I told Mrs. Raeburn, for the golden image my dear brother gave her was a present fit for a king. But we have bowed down to the golden image; yes, by Jove! and now we are sorry for it. That's—just fill my glass again, John—that's the real fact of the matter, Sheddon, and I am glad to think that you have been a spectator of all this—

seen us wash our dirty linen, as the saying
is—because it will be a lesson to you. The
real fact of the matter is, that the whole
thing has occurred through my poor brother's
ignorance of the nature of a legal contrasht
—contract. I am glad to think that under
my tutelish — tutelage — you have already
acquired sufficient knowledge of your future
profession to avoid falling into his error.
Suppose John here and yourself, who are
very good friends, I am pleased to see, were
to make a contrasht"—the attorney paused
as though he felt he had dropped something,
then hurried on as though it was not worth
while to pick it up—"the object of which
was to divide your aggregate property at
some specified future time; what would you
do to make that arrangement binding? You
would put it in writing to begin with, would
you not? You would procure witnesses;
you would purchase such a stamp as you
found on inquiry would be suitable for your
object. Well, my brother chose to dispense

with all these necessary forms, and the consequence is, he has, metaphorically speaking,
not a leg to stand on. I am, however, sorry
for him. Morally, he may have some fanciful
claim; but what have we to do with morals?
'*Fiat justitia, ruat cœlum,*'—the law must
take its course, independently of religion
and morals. But mind, Sheddon, short of
that—short of giving him half my bed, and
half my board, and cutting the horse exactly
down the middle, Alec shall have his rightsh.
He shall not be starved or snubbed; he
shall have a little pocket-money of his own;
and I tell you what"—here the attorney
placed his mouth close to my ear—"he
shall not be poisoned with that ginger wine.
And now, young gentlemen, good night;
you have had quite as much to drink as is
good for you, and I wish to be left to
meditation. It is my advice to you, ladsh,"
added he, with a flicker of a smile, "not
to make any noise that may bring Mrs.
Raeburn out to you to-night."

Of course we went upstairs at once, John on his hands and knees, not so much for silence' sake as in order grotesquely to typify enjoyment too excessive for the ordinary means of locomotion, and so to our own rooms. But I could not sleep for hours; I was haunted by Brother Alec's pale despairing face as he uttered those parting words to Gertrude, "Your poor relation will not trouble you for long!"

He had indeed looked ten years nearer to the grave when he left the room than when he had entered it. Would his hen-pecked brother, still drinking below stairs to nerve himself for the combat that awaited him, have the courage to defend him not only then, but through the days to come? or would Mrs. Raeburn push him forth into the pitiless world by slights and insults, as cruel men have pricked their enemy with spear points, and forced him over some steep place to die?

CHAPTER XII.

A CHANGE OF TREATMENT.

I SUPPOSE all of us looked for Brother Alec's appearance on the morning after that dreadful change in his position amongst us, with something of expectation. I, for my part, felt a profound pity for him; so I am sure did Gertrude, for her eyes filled with tears when he entered the breakfast-room—last of all, as it happened, with a certain gentle deprecating air (but very far from cringing), as though he felt that his existence was objected to, and would have been glad to oblige the world by leaving it.

"You are late, Mr. Alexander," said Mrs. Raeburn, severely, and looking up at the clock. "I hope this will not occur again."

"I am very sorry, madam," was the quiet reply. "For once in my life, I have a grudge against Chico." He had not brought the bird down with him as usual, lest, as I verily believe, it should receive any ill-treatment for its master's sake. "He is very restless, poor fellow, this morning, and hindered my toilette."

"That will not happen again, very often," was the cold rejoinder, "as I intend to take measures for the disposal of the bird."

Brother Alec looked up hastily, his pale face tinged with colour, and exclaimed, "I trust, madam, that whatever alteration you may think proper to make in the way of my——"

The old man hesitated, and looked confusedly at his plate, in which there was only bread and butter. The scanty dish of rashers to which we had returned was placed under Mrs. Raeburn's immediate superintendence.

"Nay," she said, curtly, "you can speak out. Of course there is, and will be, a change in your way of entertainment here. Your brother cannot afford extravagant dainties — which, after all, are very unwholesome — unless, as in Mr. Sheddon's case, a particular arrangement is entered into."

I was tolerably used to Mrs. Raeburn's bluntness by this time, but this speech of hers thoroughly overwhelmed me. I suppose I must have looked excessively disgusted, since the attorney here ventured to put in his words.

"I really do not see the necessity, Matilda, for entering into these pecuniary details."

"Do you not, Mr. Raeburn? Well, I do," she replied. "We have had quite enough of misunderstanding and misrepresentations, and in future I intend to use plain words."

If the attorney had fortified himself

against his wife's arguments the previous night, it was evident that it had been only to fall a prey to them in the morning. It was easy to see that there had been a battle royal over the body of his fallen relative, and that the lady had been the victor. Mark Raeburn had not once looked up from his plate since his brother had entered, except to greet him; while, on the other hand, Alec turned his gaze upon him with piteous persistence, as on the only quarter wherein lay his hope.

"I was about to say, Brother Mark," faltered 'he, "that, whatever new arrangements Mrs. Raeburn may think proper to make, I trust it may not be deemed necessary that I should part with the bird. It may seem foolish, and perhaps it is so, to feel so strong an attachment for a feathered creature, as I do in this case; but there are associations—so tender, Mark, that I have not ventured to allude to them even to yourself—in connection with Chico——"

"My husband has nothing to do with our domestic arrangements, Mr. Alexander," broke in Mrs. Raeburn, imperiously. "If there is any business to transact connected with your property"—and it is impossible to convey in writing the cynical stress which she laid upon that last word—"your brother is the person to apply to: but the management of this household is in my hands. I object to this poll parrot being maintained at the Priory upon many grounds; but it is only necessary to mention one—that of expense. You have told me yourself that it would be worth a hundred guineas to the proprietors of the Zoological Gardens, and I intend to write to them to offer it for that sum. If you retained it, you would be expending no less than five pounds a year, interest of money, in its maintenance—or rather we should be expending that sum—not to mention that it costs in nuts and oranges as much per week as, by the statistical accounts of missionary enterprise, would convert an

African adult from darkness to spiritual light. No, Mr. Alexander, the bird will not remain in this house."

Brother Alec looked towards Brother Mark, but looked in vain. The attorney was chasing a piece of rasher of bacon round his plate, as the Queen's Hunt chases a stag, not with the object of devouring it, but merely for the sake of the occupation; he did not dare to meet that piteous gaze, so pregnant with reproachful memories.

"With your permission, Mrs. Raeburn," exclaimed Gertrude, hurriedly, "if cousin Alec must needs dispose of Chico, I will buy the bird myself and also maintain it at my own charge."

"Bravo, bravo!" cried John, pounding the table with the handle of his knife. "You're a brick, Gerty!"

John's expressions were certainly very vulgar, but the sentiment they conveyed was, in this case, irreproachable. I think

I never liked him so well as I did at that moment.

"Be silent, sir," cried his mother, angrily. "Your manners are those of a ——," she was obviously going to say "of a public-house," but reflecting that the metaphor was itself a little coarse, she corrected herself hastily, with "are not those of a private house. No one would think that your schooling had cost your parents eighty pounds per annum, exclusive of extras." Thus she continued to upbraid her hopeful son, not so much, I fancy, for his moral behoof, as to gain time in which to revolve Gertrude's proposition in her mind.

Brother Alec's eyes had flashed one grateful look at the young girl, then once more fixed themselves on his brother's face.

"No, Gertrude," said Mrs. Raeburn, suddenly breaking off in her lecture, "your proposal cannot be seriously entertained. My husband would not, I am sure, as your guardian, consent to the expenditure of so vast a sum upon a feathered fowl" (she laid a great stress on feathered, as though, if the bird had been an apteryx, he would have consented at once); "it is utterly out of the question."

"I have the money of my own," observed Gertrude, quietly, "and so need not trouble my cousin."

"How can you have the money?" inquired Mrs. Raeburn, always interested in the subject of the acquisition of property. "Where did you get it from?"

Gertrude blushed and hesitated. "I shall sell the golden image which cousin Alec was so good as to give me," said she; "with a little saving of my allowance added to what that will bring, I could easily get the hundred pounds. Then the bird, you know, cousin Alec," added she, softly, "would be as much your gift as the other."

But the old man only cast down his eyes upon his plate, and uttered not a word.

"My dear Gertrude, it is not a question of mere money," broke in Mrs. Raeburn, loftily, "it is one of principle."

"Then it's all up with Chico," murmured John, with sagacious intuition. It was always "all up" with everything that was pleasant (and not profitable) when his mother took high moral grounds.

"I would rather wring the neck of the bird with my own hands," she continued, "than abet such abominable extravagance. The parrot and serpents will, of course, go together. As for the bull-dog, which has already consumed in this house sufficient food to keep a Christian family of six persons at the rate of a quarter of a pound of meat apiece per week (for I have calculated it), I shall send to Mr. Welsh, the butcher's, with my compliments. I have heard him express admiration for it, and since I am certain he cheated us in his last joint, he quite deserves it. I shall get you, John, to take it round."

"I'm hanged if I do!" exclaimed John,

resolutely. "Take it round, indeed! Do
you mean, take it round the neck and pull
it there? Why, it would be as much as my
life's worth. That beast always looks at me
as though he was hungry."

"I will take Fury to the butcher's, if
such is your wish, Mrs. Raeburn," observed
Brother Alec, quickly.

"Very good, Mr. Alexander; it is in-
different to me who takes him," was the
ungracious rejoinder, "so long as he goes;"
and with that she rose from the table.

It was plain that his sister-in-law was
unappeasable; never had I beheld any woman
so bitter towards a person of the opposite
sex. In the pleasure which she manifestly
took in giving him pain, she reminded me
of · that character common enough (to the
shame of our educational system) in the
English boy-world, but which, considering
the youth of the offender, and what ought
to be youth's attributes, is a most loathsome
one—the school-bully. In all that she did

thenceforth she could scarcely have proceeded
more openly to make her relative's life a
burthen to him, if she had told him that
such was her intention in so many words.
Only in the presence of strangers she still
used to him a forced style of civility, since
it was of importance to conceal the change
in their relations.   Of course there were no
more dinner-parties at the Priory, but invitations came more than once for Mr. and
Mrs. Raeburn, and Mr. Alexander Raeburn,
which she strove hard to make her brother-
in-law accept ; but in this one respect he
was firm in resisting her will.

"I would do anything in my power,
madam, to please you, and make up for the
disappointment of which I have been the
involuntary cause : but to go out to dinner
is not in my power.   I could not for a
moment play my part as you would have
me play it."

To look at him, so old, and worn, and
broken, and to hear his trembling voice,

was to be convinced of this fact. Mrs. Raeburn forbore to insist upon a proceeding which would have certainly had the contrary effect to that she desired; he therefore wrote to decline all such hospitalities on the ground of physical indisposition—a very warrantable plea, though his disease was scarcely one to be remedied by the doctor, even in the unimaginable case of Mrs. Raeburn's invoking his aid. So she and the attorney went out to dine alone, much to the disgust of the inviters; while Brother Alec stayed at home with us "young people." Gertrude and I were, of course, full of sympathy for him; and I am bound to say that John behaved with far better feeling than I had given him credit for. He ceased to mimic him, addressed him personally with great respect, and spoke of him in his absence with compassion, as "that unfortunate old buffer." But none of us could win poor Brother Alec from his woe. So soon as he had dispatched his scanty meal—

for when the heads of the family were out, the board at the Priory had even less cause to " groan " than usual—he would retire to his own room, where, far into the night, I could hear him talking in melancholy accents to Chico, and that sympathetic bird replying in the same key.

When " carriage people," as Mrs. Raeburn always described those of her acquaintances who possessed vehicles of their own, came to make kind inquiries after the invalid, he always denied himself to them; and to hear that lady make excuses for his non-appearance, was, if her son happened to be present, always a situation of great embarrassment to me. The effort it cost her to frame words of sympathy about her pauper-relative; the expression of her face, as she did so; the thanks she returned for the hopes expressed that he would soon " be himself again," were all reproduced, as in a mirror, for my benefit by the irrepressible John. If the theory of " natural selection " could be

proved by a single example, it was established in his proper person (though not
quite in the sense attached to it by Darwin),
since it seemed as if, out of his own will
and pleasure, he had transmogrified himself
from man to monkey.

What heightened the attraction of this
spectacle was the fact that—though of course,
quite ignorant of the true circumstances of
the case—these sympathising callers, who
were mostly of the fashionable sort, were
themselves incredulous of Mrs. Raeburn's
sincerity ; they thought that she was count-
ing upon Brother Alec's illness terminating
fatally and in a magnificent legacy. One
of these visitors, however, was very different
from the rest, namely, my Uncle Hastings.
He had ridden over from the Rectory,
directly he heard of the old man's indisposition, partly out of his own regard for
him, partly urged by my aunt's entreaties :
" Pray do go and look after the poor man ;
it is my belief that those people are killing

him amongst them for the sake of his money." And though the invalid had made no exceptions in his refusal to see anybody, the rector would not be denied. "I am a friend of thirty years' standing," said he, "and if Alec Raeburn is not well enough to come down and see me, I will go upstairs and see him." And he did so.

The interview between them was a long one, and when the rector returned to the drawing-room his face was very grave. Mrs Raeburn's mind was evidently disturbed. She had a suspicion, I think, that he had been told everything, and assumed a somewhat defiant air.

"Well, Mr. Hastings, and what do you think of Mr. Alexander?"

"I think your brother-in-law seriously ill, madam. I do not hesitate to say that his appearance shocked me; so great a change within so short a time I never saw in any man."

Mrs. Raeburn sighed heavily, from sympathy, as the rector doubtless imagined, but, as I conjectured, from the relief his words had given her.

"Yes, indeed," said she; "but I trust he is not so bad as he looks. He has really no serious symptoms, except want of appetite. Nothing seems to tempt him." (Here John's face became a picture, which somehow reproduced "scrap pie" and un-attractive cutlets). "He has expressed no wish for medical advice."

"Perhaps not, but he surely ought to have it; at least, if I were in your case, I should insist upon having a professional opinion. I would rather have such a re-sponsibility upon the doctor's shoulders than on mine. Dr. Wilde, I hear," (this was our new practitioner at Kirkdale) "makes the diseases of old age quite a speciality, and he seems very clever."

"My brother-in-law has only to express the wish to have it gratified," returned Mrs. Raeburn, icily.

"Of course, of course, my dear madam; of that I am certain; but don't you think it should be suggested to him? I don't wish to frighten you, I'm sure; Alec's appearance, it is true, is peculiar, his white beard on his white face makes him look, doubtless, worse than he is; but my advice is, let him see the doctor."

My uncle's behaviour was, I thought, a little dictatorial, but he was a man accustomed to have his own way with everybody, except his wife; her means gave him importance, his personal popularity was great, and being at once squire and parson of his own parish, he was wont to give advice with authority. Mrs. Raeburn had reasons of her own, as I afterwards came to know, for not getting into a passion with the rector, and no glow from the fire that was doubtless burning within her was permitted to be seen without.

"It is like yourself, Mr. Hastings, to take so warm an interest in your old friend,"

answered she slowly; "but you must remember that he is Mark's own brother, and
that my husband is not one to neglect his
own flesh and blood."

"Indeed, indeed, Mrs. Raeburn, you
mistake me," replied the rector. "I am
quite aware of Mark's kindness of heart,
and can easily imagine that Alec himself is
the chief obstacle to the proposition I would
suggest; but his objection to have medical
advice should be overborne. It is for the
very reason that he is so near of kin to you
that I have ventured to speak; since, if
anything were to happen to him, and Mark
were greatly benefited by it—and ordinary
precautions had been neglected—Don't you
see, my good woman?" explained my uncle,
falling into his parochial visiting style.

"Dear me, I never thought of that," said
Mrs. Raeburn, with innocent surprise.

"Of course not; your conscience would
have nothing to reproach itself with, doubtless. I only wished to put you on your

guard, that you should not give the world an opportunity of being censorious."

"You are most kind," answered Mrs. Raeburn. "I will speak to my brother-in-law on the subject at once. Good morning."

"Now, upon my word," said my uncle, as I dutifully accompanied him to the town where he had left his horse, "that woman is not so black as she is painted. Some people would have flown out in a rage when I suggested that, if Alec died, folks would say she had killed her brother-in-law to get his money."

"I don't think you did quite say that, uncle."

"No; but she knew what I meant well enough. She's as sharp as a razor, and very reasonable too, that I must allow. When one comes to know people, and when anything of importance causes them to speak out to you, I have always found that there is some good in everybody."

It did not become me to dispute the dictum of so experienced an ecclesiastic; and as to the particular case of my hostess, perhaps my six months' acquaintance with her had been insufficient to develop her merits, so I said nothing on that point. My curiosity, on the other hand, was considerable as to whether the invalid had in any way made a confidant of the rector.

"And do you really think Mr. Alexander's indisposition is serious, uncle?"

"Well, yes, I do. He not only looks ill, but is utterly down in the mouth and hipped. If one could see inside him, I expect you would find his liver about three times its proper size, or else gone altogether. If your aunt saw him (here the rector chuckled), she would say that 'those Raeburns were poisoning him.'"

"Did he say that he was not comfortable at the Priory?"

"Oh dear no! Indeed, our talk was almost exclusively of old times; his only complaint was, that he was afraid he was about to lose his parrot. I suppose it has got the pip or something, though it looked to me well enough."

"He didn't tell you about Mrs. Raeburn's sending away his dog?"

"Not a word. Why, the brute was in his room, large as life and larger."

"Yes; the butcher, to whom it was sent as a present, sent it back again. It frightened people from the shop, he said, and eat half a sheep or so a day."

"I don't wonder," laughed my uncle. "It was like giving a man a white elephant. It must be expensive as well as inconvenient to keep poor Alec's menagerie; but his relatives will be well paid for it some day, and I am afraid only too soon."

Dissimulation was an art unknown to my uncle, and I felt certain that he was concealing nothing from me; it was clear, therefore, that the invalid had kept his griefs locked up in his own bosom.

CHAPTER XIII.

THE ACCUSATION.

ALTHOUGH I have spoken of Brother Alec as an invalid, he was not such in the ordinary acceptation of the term; for although he denied himself to guests, he came down to every meal, and was treated in every respect as usual by his hostess, which, I am sorry to say, was with no respect at all. It was not to be expected that much fuss should be made about a "poor relation," who felt a little out of sorts, but it seemed shameful that her tongue should be just as rancorous against the poor old gentleman, in his present depressed and feeble state, as though he had been in good health. Even the school-bully holds his hand when his victim is sick.

"So, Mr. Alexander," observed Mrs. Raeburn at dessert that evening, and immediately after the servant had withdrawn, "you have been telling pretty tales to Mr. Hastings, I hear."

This was evidently a feeler; some suspicion probably still lingering in her mind that the rector might have learnt more than he chose to tell.

"Tales, madam? I had no tales to tell," answered poor Brother Alec, in tones that, for all my pity for him, reminded me of the needy knife-grinder in Canning's ballad.

"Oh, indeed," was the snappish reply; "then I suppose Mr. Hastings invented them. You want to see the doctor, it seems, and make complaints that your wish has not been anticipated."

"Indeed, madam, there is some mistake. I never expressed any such wish to Mr. Hastings. No doctor would do me any good; no, no." The pathos of his words, which pierced every heart but one, only added fuel, I could see, to Mrs. Raeburn's fire; but he went on unconsciously of that, with his humble apology. "'There is nothing the matter with me, Hastings,' I said. 'I am not ill.'"

"You look ill then," exclaimed his hostess with acerbity, "and that is exceedingly unpleasant. 'Why doesn't he cut off that dreadful beard,' said Mr. Hastings, 'which makes our friend look so ghastly.' I wish you would, Mr. Alexander; I have always said I disliked it." Cruel and insolent as were her words, the voice and manner with which she spoke them were even still more harsh.

A faint flush crept over the old man's white face, as he cast—it was very rarely that he did so now — a mute appealing glance at his brother.

Mark shuffled in his chair uneasily.

"Matilda, I think you are going too

far," he said, "in meddling with my brother
Alec.   It cannot make any difference to
you whether he wears a beard or not.   He
is not *your* husband—eh, Alec ?" (here
the attorney gave a ghost of a laugh).
"He is old enough, my dear, to choose
for himself, whether he shall shave or not,
I suppose."

"I only echoed Mr. Hastings's very
reasonable remark," replied Mrs. Raeburn,
more mildly ; not influenced probably so
much by her husband's appeal, as moved
for the moment by the displeasure evident
in Gertrude's face, and the disgust (I hope)
expressed by my own.   "A beard, as I
always said, does not become Mr. Alexander ;
and in every case it is an outlandish and
unnecessary appendage.   People of position
can, of course, be as eccentric in their
appearance as they please ; but that is
certainly not your brother's case.   I have
heard you say, myself, that it is absurd in
the chemist's assistant to wear moustachios.

I mean nothing offensive, but I object to it on principle, as incongruous and unseemly. Of course Mr. Alexander will do as he likes, but I have expressed my sentiments."

Here Gertrude rose from her chair in indignant protest; it was her intention to have walked straight out of the room in sign that she would be no longer witness to her cousin's humiliation; but Mrs. Raeburn, affecting to misunderstand her, and to have herself given the signal for retreat, rose with her, and they quitted the apartment together.

"Mark," said Brother Alec, "you heard what your wife has said to me; what am I to do?"

His voice, though gentle, was very steady; more so than it ever had been since the change had occurred in his position in the house.

The attorney helped himself to a whole glass of brandy—he made no stranger of his brother now in that respect—and then answered, " I should please myself, Alec. You heard what I said to Matilda. I would say as much again and more. It is I who have prevented her sending away your parrot. I had a great fight for that, and she is at me about it almost every night.".

" Do not make your life unhappy on my account, Mark," was the quiet rejoinder. " You mean me well, but you are not strong enough to help me. How can I expect it, when you cannot even help yourself ? "

" I don't know what you mean, Alec," replied the attorney, with an angry flush. " I am master in my own house, I hope. But, of course, there are some things in which one's wife will have her way; at least, that is so in England, however matters are managed in Peru."

" I see," said the other coldly.

" You say ' you see,' my dear Alec," laughed the attorney, on whom the liquor had begun to have an effect, " as if seeing

was not believing; but was it not so? Did
you not find your Peruvian wife rather inclined to take the bit in her mouth, eh, like
Matilda?"

"My wife is dead, Mark. When alive,
she was quite a different person from my
sister-in-law."

"Well, you see, you don't hit it off,
you two; and it's a sad pity. Matilda is
naturally masterful, and you, having no profession, are always at home with her, and
liable to her little onslaughts. It's a good
thing for a married man to have a calling,
if it's only that it gives him a loophole
through which he can make himself scarce
occasionally. I could defend you well enough
—I've proved it to-night—if I could be
always by, Alec; but I have no doubt she
worries you when I am away. As for your
beard—I say again she has no business to
dictate such a thing—but if I were in your
place, and loved peace and quietness better,
I'd cut it off. Then, perhaps, she will be

pacified, and not pitch into me again for a night or two about the bird."

The unreserve with which the attorney was accustomed to discuss his domestic affairs, and especially when he had been taking his favourite liquor, had long ceased to astonish me; but I had never heard him confess his wife's supremacy so openly as on this occasion. I think he had nerved himself thus to acquaint his brother, once for all, that he was powerless to help him. The little show of bitterness which the other had made in that "she was quite a different person from my sister-in-law," had annoyed the hen-pecked man and supplied him with the fillip he needed, and he effected his object, since to my knowledge Brother Alec never made appeal or remonstrance to him again.

Except in matters relating to his own profession, wherein Mark was singularly discreet, and indeed so reticent in communicating them that I suppose no articled clerk ever learned less law than I did during the space of time that I remained under his tutorship, he was, as I have said, by nature open and unreserved; this characteristic was shared by his son John, in whom it was even heightened by a total want of percep- tion of the necessity of concealment; while Mrs. Raeburn, from long habit of despotic rule, rode rough-shod over everybody, and gave herself no trouble to put the velvet glove on her iron fingers. Thus it happened that, though but a youthful student of human nature, the proceedings of the Raeburn family —for poor Brother Alec was a character one might run and read—and even their motives, were as clear to me as though I had been a Machiavelli. Nor was Gertrude Floyd any enigma to me by this time; although no vows had been interchanged between us, I felt myself secure of her affections, and fondly hoped that only patience was needed on my part to enjoy a happiness of which I never- theless acknowledged myself undeserving. Every day brought for me some new proof

—such as that tacit but pointed remonstrance she had made against the treatment of her poor cousin—of her generosity and spirit; and I watched her ripening charms of mind and body as the child watches the peach that has been promised to him ripening on the garden wall, without a thought of the canker-worm, or of the thief. Indeed who could be the thief in this case, even in design, save the volatile John, of whose rivalship I knew I need entertain no fears.

Thus then stood matters at the Priory, when a circumstance occurred which placed the unhappy dependent on his brother's bounty in even a more humiliating position than he had yet occupied, while it also threatened to deprive him of the sympathy entertained for him by those who claimed to be his friends. This sympathy was just then at its height, since the poor fellow had actually submitted to the personal degradation suggested by his implacable hostess, and parted with his venerable beard. I am aware of the ludicrous ideas that such a sacrifice cannot but suggest. " The manly growth that fringed his chin " is a line which tries the gravity of even the readers of an epic ; and how, therefore, is it possible to make such matters serious in plain prose ? Yet the personal indignity inflicted on Brother Alec, considering his age, and kinship, and forlorn condition, was as great as it is possible to conceive, and stirred the indignation of all beholders—fortunately by this time confined to the family circle. There was one feature in the case that might have made even Mrs. Raeburn herself, had she not been as emotionless as a millstone— namely, that the change thus wrought in the old man's appearance brought out his likeness to her son in the most extraordinary manner. The lines and wrinkles in the old man's face were already mirrored in that of the young one, produced there, I fancy, partly by his tricks of grimacing ; and now that the dignity which the beard always gives to the aged was gone, there was really little but the grey head—except that the depressed and broken manner contrasted strongly enough with John's upstart and graceless ways—to distinguish uncle from nephew.

However, "Well, Mr. Alexander, I call that a great improvement; you really do look now like a civilised being," was all the remark that the old man's compliance with her wishes drew from his sister-in-law. If he had hoped to conciliate her by his obedience he was mistaken indeed.

A few days after this a letter arrived by the afternoon's post for Mrs. Racburn, the contents of which (for it happened that she received it at the dinner-table) appeared to all eyes to disturb her exceedingly.

"What is it, Matilda?" inquired the attorney anxiously. He was always anxious about letters, but of late months I had noticed that this habit had greatly increased with him. He did not drink more than usual in my presence, but I had a suspicion that he had taken to do so more and more in private, and that his nerves were beginning to be affected.

"Never mind just now, Mark; you will all hear soon enough," was his wife's reply, delivered in her most frigid tone; and presently, when the servant had left the room, we did hear.

"Mr. Alexander," said she, with stately calm, "I have received a communication within the last half hour which concerns you nearly, and myself in a more remote degree. Am I favoured, sir, with your attention?"

This question, which was shot out with amazing sharpness, startled Brother Alec not a little. He had grown so accustomed to be the object of his sister-in-law's remarks, which partook largely of the style of a judge's address to the prisoner at the bar, and always ended in a pretty severe sentence, that he rarely raised his head

when she addressed him, but he looked up
now with a grave and deprecating air, and
said, "I am quite at your service, madam,
I assure you."

"So you say, sir, and so you would
have others believe, I know. It is part of
your plan to be always submissive and
yielding. It has brought you a great deal
of sympathy in this house, and which, no
doubt, you also intended, considerable oppro-
brium upon myself. As for me, however,
I have cared nothing for that, since I have
been actuated solely by a sense of duty.
I made a tolerably correct guess at your
character when I first set eyes upon you."

"Matilda!" exclaimed the attorney in
mild expostulation, for either from weak-
ness or want of will he now hardly held
up the shield at all between his brother
and these cruel darts. "Matilda, I am surprised at you."

"You will be more surprised at that
man there"—and she stretched out her

skinny arm and pointed to Brother Alec
across the table—"when I have told you
what I have just now heard about him. I
have incurred much odium, I say, upon
this gentleman's account, because I read
him from the first, and was therefore not
disposed to spoil and humour him. I have
never permitted him—and I am now most
thankful to say it—to have his own way
in this house, though, I trust, I have
not forgotten that he was my husband's
brother."

"A little more than kin and less than
kind," murmured Brother Alec softly.

"I daresay," continued Mrs. Raeburn
contemptuously, "you would not be so
glib with your quotations, sir, if you knew
what was coming." Her dislike of her
poor relative was so excessive that she could
not prevent herself from flying at him in
this cat-like manner, which seriously com-
promised the dignity of her judicial tone.
"The time has come, Mr. Alexander," she

continued, more solemnly, "for the correctness of my judgment to be established. It seems that we have not only harboured an impostor in this house, Mark, in the person of your injured brother yonder, but a common thief."

An exclamation of horror broke from every lip save that of the accused. The colour came into his face, as it had often done under his sister-in-law's insults, and his thin white hands, which were peeling an orange—it had been the smallest on the dish, and had a spot of green mould upon it—trembled excessively; but he did not even lift his eyes.

"This is monstrous, Matilda; there must be some mistake," ejaculated the attorney.

"Mistake!" echoed she, with a bitter laugh. "Look at the man, sitting there without a word to say for himself, and judge for yourselves."

"I will answer for him, Mrs. Raeburn," exclaimed Gertrude, boldly. "If it be a mistake, or if it be not a mistake, it is a falsehood."

"I am quite of Miss Floyd's opinion," said I. "It is a most infamous charge, whoever made it."

"It's worse than that," observed John; "it's actionable; and you had better look out, mother."

Mrs. Raeburn regarded us with complacent contempt.

"The mistake, or falsehood, as you so delicately put it, Gertrude, is at least none of mine," said she; "you shall hear whose it is, then judge whether it is likely to be correct or not. Three or four days ago I wrote to the Zoological Society in London, offering to dispose of a Peruvian Night-Parrot; and this is the official reply I received this afternoon:

"'MADAM,—In reply to your communication of the 15th instant, I am instructed to acquaint you that the bird of which you speak is already the property of the

Zoological Society, from whom it was stolen
some six months ago. It should have arrived
at Southampton by "The Java"'—the vessel
you came in, I believe, Mr. Alexander—'on
the 18th of October last. The parrot had
been bespoken from Peru, and our agent
went down to the port in order to receive
it, but found——

"That the bird had flown," interpolated
the irrepressible John, in close imitation of
his mother's manner.

"Silence, sir!" exclaimed she, so vehe-
mently, that John fell back in his chair with
the air—a trifle exaggerated—of a gentleman
who has been shot through the head.

"'But found that the bird had been
already conveyed away by a passenger.
You are quite correct as to its value, and
it is the fixed determination of the Society
to recover their property. Your brother-
in-law, they have no doubt, received it in
ignorance that it had been unlawfully come
by; but unless it is instantly restored to

them, without charge and with a satisfactory explanation of how he became possessed of it, they will be compelled to communicate with the police. Should any accident happen to the bird in the meantime, they will hold him responsible in the sum of one hundred pounds.'

"You will not deny, I suppose, Mr. Alexander, that you were the passenger who took that bird away from the ship?"

"Mark," said Brother Alec, softly, "your wife asks me whether I am a thief. Can you not answer for me, even that far?"

"Of course, my dear Alec, of course; but why can't you answer for yourself? Nothing can surely be easier. It's a simple question of fact, you know."

With a gentle sigh the old man turned to his hostess, "If, then, I needs must say so, madam, I did not steal the bird."

"Do not prevaricate, sir. I did not ask you that question. What I asked was, Were you not the passenger referred to, who brought that parrot from the ship?"

"I was, madam; but I did not steal it."

"That is another subterfuge. Can you account for its possession? How came you by the bird? Can you tell us that?" And Mrs. Raeburn looked around her triumphantly; she piqued herself on her powers of cross-examination, before which many a domestic had succumbed in tears.

"You wish to hear how I came by Chico?" answered the old man, quietly. "Nay, madam; I will not tell you that."

"You will not? That means you dare not!"

Brother Alec's pale face worked convulsively. It was some time before he found voice to say:

"You have my answer, madam, and it is final."

"Very good, sir, perhaps you will be more communicative to the police. The parrot will be sent to-morrow morning to

its rightful owners. I am sorry, for your
sake, that the serpents have been destroyed
(she had caused boiling water to be poured
into their boxes through the hole in the lid),
since a donation of them might have been
considered in the way of amends. As to
an explanation of how you became possessed
of the bird, I have only one to offer."

"But, Mrs. Raeburn——" appealed Gertrude.

"No, Gertrude, I must decline to listen
to you. The matter is too serious to be
made the subject of sentimental interference. If, as I guess, you were about to
propose to pay the hundred pounds for this
worthless fellow, I will not permit it; that
would be, as my husband will tell you, to
compound a felony. The Zoological Society
may, perhaps, be content with the restitu-
tion of their property; but I am not going
to run the risk of seeing the officers of the
law enter my doors in search of a felon.
After to-day, your brother will find a home

for himself elsewhere. He shall stay no longer under this roof."

"But this is being very precipitate, Matilda," remonstrated the attorney.

"Precipitate do you call it, Mr. Raeburn, when this man has been our guest here the better part of a year—eating and drinking of the best! It was through my weakly yielding to your wishes that I have harboured him so long, not to mention his bird, which is not his, it seems, nor ever has been. I must assert myself for once, Mark, as the mistress of this house. You must take your choice between your wife and him; for either he or I leave this roof to-morrow."

There was not much doubt as to which of the two would have to go.

END OF VOL. I.

CHARLES DICKENS AND EVANS, CRYSTAL PALACE PRESS.